MYSTiFIED BY STEPHANIE

By

Daniel A. Shea

ISBN: 0692160329
ISBN-13: 978-0-692-16032-9

DEDICATION

I dedicate this book to war fighters, special forces (all branches) traditional and non-traditional spooks. The men and women who leave their families to go abroad to scrape the forces of evil off our planet. To the American fighters who never make it home. And to the Talking Heads for timeless music.

Kudos to you and May God Continue to Shine a Light on Your Path!

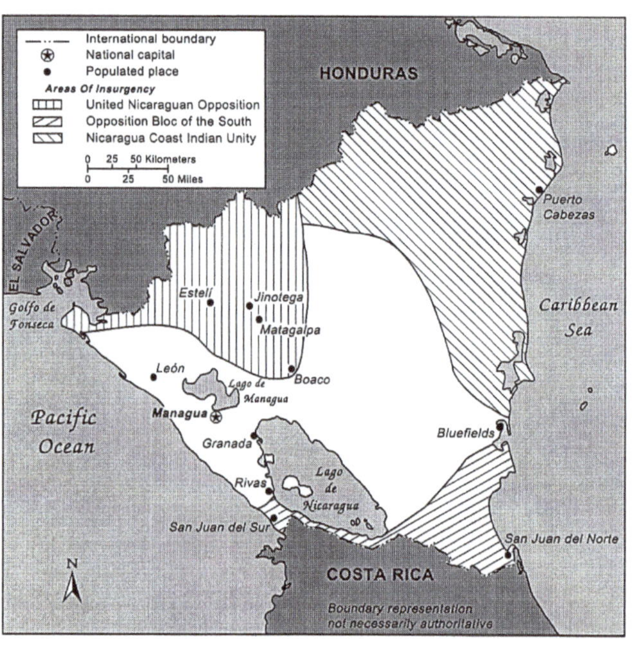
International boundary
National capital
Populated place
Areas Of Insurgency
United Nicaraguan Opposition
Opposition Bloc of the South
Nicaragua Coast Indian Unity
0 25 50 Kilometers
0 25 50 Miles
HONDURAS
EL SALVADOR
Golfo de Fonseca
Estelí
Jinotega
Matagalpa
León
Boaco
Lago de Managua
Managua
Pacific Ocean
Granada
Rivas
Lago de Nicaragua
San Juan del Sur
Puerto Cabezas
Caribbean Sea
Bluefields
San Juan del Norte
COSTA RICA
Boundary representation not necessarily authoritative
N

HOW THE IRAN-CONTRA STORY LEAKED

(b)(3)(c)

With all the publicity surrounding the Iran-Contra affair, there was little focus on who leaked the initial story to the Lebanese newspaper *Al-Shiraa* on 1-2 November 1986, or why. It was not until June 1987 that reporting was received on the origin of the mysterious press piece. According to (b)(1) (b)(3)(n) Damascus leaked the US-Iranian arms-for-hostages deal for its own purposes, thus setting in motion events that would temporarily undermine US prestige in the Middle East, expose the diversion of funds to the Nicaraguan Contras, and create a major controversy in US politics.

(b)(1) (b)(3)(n) the Syrian Government first learned of the arms-for-hostages deal from its chargé in Tehran, Iyad Mahmud, who probably got the information through his contacts in the Iranian Government. For Mahmud, who was in fact a Syrian military intelligence officer, this knowledge quickly became a dangerous thing.

In early October 1986, a group of Iranian officials kidnaped Mahmud and beat him badly before letting him go. Iranian press reports at the time claimed that Mahmud had been arrested by the Iranian antivice squad for drunkenness in the company of women and then released 24 hours later. This story covered up the real reason for the arrest—to intimidate Mahmud from passsing on his knowledge of the deal.

Immediately after Mahmud's release, Damascus withdrew him, and he apparently then told his colleagues what he knew. claims that Syria, now angry at both the US and Iran, chose the Syrian-financed *Al-Shiraa* to print the story. Although Syrian intelligence officials tried to take credit for disrupting US relations throughout the region, they evidently never anticipated how far-reaching the political reaction would be in the US. (b)(1) (b)(3)(n)

Why Syria Did It

Syria was the only Arab state to consistently back Iran in the Persian Gulf War from 1980 to 1988, and, in return, Iran provided Syria with low-priced oil. In this context, Damascus had no reason to stop the US sale of weapons to Tehran. While Damascus may have feared further US-Iranian cooperation on the Lebanese civil war and other issues, such cooperation is difficul(b)(1) to imagine. Yet claims that Syria exposed the deal out of its anger at botl(b)(3)(n) the US and Iran. One possible explanation is that Mahmud found out about the role Israel played in facilitating the deal and that Damascus feared Israeli-Iranian ties would return to the relationship of the 1970s, when Israel provide a steady flow of weapons to the Shah of Iran. But Syrian knowledge of the Israeli angle was unlikely, considering that the *Al-Shiraa* piece made no mention of it. A less unlikely explanation is that Syria had the story printed to punish Iran for its treatment of Mahmud.

(b)(1) (b)(3)(n) however, may have been misled by his Syrian sources on Syrian motivations for releasing the story. He did not account for the four-week lapse between early

1762

UNCLASSIFIED

C 09526

Transcription of Sam Geneva notes

1. The initial meeting with [redacted] was between just he and Sam on 8
November. [redacted] had several points to make in this initial meeting. He
wanted to re[...] us that Montazari is a moderate who had been duped by those
around him. [...] recommended that we base our judgement on his public
statements [...] to the media on various subjects. He is well liked by
the media. [...] greatest strength is his ability as a public
speaker. [...] from [redacted] statements that he is either an advisor
of Mont[...] or in [...] is involved with his politically.
2. [...] interrupted at this point and said he wanted to tell Sam that he
was to[...] Tehran to have nothing to do with the CIA rep in the group.
said t[...] indicate that there is some danger in his meeting with Sam.

Sam belie[...] comes out again we may have something. [...] told him
that if thi[...] goes forward It is going to be up to [redacted] and Sam. It
is essential that we have better info on what is going on in Tehran so that we
make no miscalculations or do something which would unknowingly endanger the
Rafsenjani faction. We agreed that we will have to spend a lot of time
together at the next meeting, if there is a next meeting.
3. [redacted] is very much concerned about the Gorbanifar-Khashoggi-Israeli
connection. He said that their intelligence people had taken a hard look at
these connections and concluded that Gorbanifar is an Israeli agent. They are
uncertain as to what to do about it and are open to suggestions from us. He
said that they had decided not to try t[...] him back to Tehran. In order to
appease him and keep him quiet they int[...] continue to buy some items from
him. (note; he said all this before th[...] spread revelations began so there
may be a change). He would like to d[...] the Gorbanifar problem at the next
meeting. Sam pointed out that Gorbani[...] [redacted]
[redacted] [...] ted that we should not make
things too tough for Gorbanifar. He a[...] we could do something via the
Israelis?
4. [redacted]

5. [redacted] wanted us to know that the Shera newspaper in Beirut was under
Syrian control. This has led some in Tehran to conclude that the U.S. might
have had a hand in the expose. Sam pointed out to him that we h[...] considerable
information which clearly indicates that Hizbullah is involved [...]
newspaper. We had concluded that Mehdi Hashemi may have used [...]
of channelling his leak. [redacted]

UNCLASSIFIED

Partially Declassified/Released [...]
under provisions of E.O. 12356
by B. Reger, National Security Council

C11N 4031

4460

TS 87-0106
Copy 3 of

1763

6. Later on 8 November [redacted] gave a kind of pep speech to the American
delegation in which he emphasized the need to forget the past and move on to a
new relationship. He said that because of the nature of the government in
Tehran, we should look at things as if we are dealing with a coorporate
structure. He also said that they were somewhat disappointed in the
Frankfurt meetings as they had hoped to move ahead faster on the intel
exchange. He also complained about the Israelis and said that we should have
moved to [...] them and Gorbanifar. He argued that the Gorbanifar
problem [...] one that we should have solved. He also tried to
argue [...] the leaks had started in the west. He even
sugg[...] that some [...] ir people thought that the leaks were engineered by
CIA [...] some undefined purpose and this convinced them that CIA did not know
what [...] doing. In short he tried in the best Iranian fashion to fault our
side [...] everything that had gone wrong. He added that the current situation
in T[...] very [...] is such that we must understand that it was a near
mirac[...] they [...] able to avoid a serious confrontation with the
leftis[...] the celebrations on the occasion of the aniversary of
the tak[...] embassy. He summed up by saying that this was the most
difficult [...] ever undertaken. He was under impossible pressure. We
must understand that he is the only true friend that we have. We should be
sincere with him and develop mutual trust between us. He emphasised teamwork
and we should now work together.

C 09527

UNCLASSIFIED

7. [redacted]

8. On 9 Nov., North began by sayin[...] he had specific instructions to
discuss certain things with [redacted] on [...] lease of Jacobsen, the 17 prisoners
in Kuwait and views on how we proceed [...] ly. North spent some time in
describing the situation in Washington [...] emphasized that we were doing our
best to protect Rafsenjani and the bu[...] relationship between our two
countries. Press commentary based on [...] njani's speech has hurt. Although
we are maintaining a no comment postu[...] pressures are mounting. Our problem
is at one time to find ways to protect [...] relationship and at the same time
find ways to move it along. We must [...] better information on what is going
on in Iran so that we are confronted w[...] no suprises. One example is the
photographic copies of the [redacted] passports. If these are published we will be
in deep trouble. [redacted] comment on this was "are you sure that photographs
were actually taken?" He said not to worry that he would make sure that no
Photos were turned over to anyone. We said fine but if all else fails, give
us some prior warning.

9. North stated that we were anxious to go ahead as soon as the hostage
issue is behind us. We have a commo package, and have also identified a
technician. We definitly do not want any of this to appear on television as
we do not wish to endanger the technician when and if we send him [...] North
added that he wishes to emphasize that he is here at the order [...]
President and we still have the same objectives as explained [...] ton and
Frankfurt. Our problem as we now see it is that we must get [...] s out
in order to get the press off our backs.

UNCLASSIFIED

C11N 4031

TS 87-0106
Copy 3 of __

ACKNOWLEDGMENTS

While some people struggle with gender identity I struggle with being a civilian vice a military officer. As a teenager I was supposed to serve as a U.S. Marine. While other little kids played Army – Yes you guessed it I was playing MARINES! I was to be lifelong career officer. Starting as a Drill Sergeant and to work my way up and become the first Five Star General of the Corps. This was supposed to be my calling. Dedication, Loyalty, God, Country, Family Oorah!! A first class warrior!

If you think about it God took a long time to free the Israelites from Egypt. Who has time to wait for one plague after another back in the day? One golden arrow and a good shot would've done the job.

However, it was not my deck of cards serve as a Marine. It didn't get me down. Well it did get me down. But I didn't think to suicide over it. There is no reason to suicide should life not go your way. Just stick out as it will get better. But you my fellow reader if you really must…

"You may find yourself, living in a shotgun shack, and you may find yourself in another part of the world, and you may find yourself behind the wheel of a large automobile, and you may find yourself in a beautiful house, with a beautiful wife and you may ask yourself, well, how did I get here?"

But first train yourself, learn to climb, run, fight, shoot, zero out and read up on tricks of the trade. Practice your skills and test them. Read maps, and have extra rental cars. Learn how to blend in, learn escape and evasion. Become an international courier or find a way to fund your one way international vacation to foreign lands. Learn a few languages and last but not least – learn lip reading. God I can't stand listening to everyone's private conversation. Use your credit card cash advance to stock up on hunting gear. When you're ready BAM! Lights out on a few Hitler, Mussolini, and Stalin dictator types.

Also, read up and identify their supporters (think Gerald Bull) Oorah Yut!!!! There will be less genocide in the world and you will have serve a life worth living. Just complete the mission and may God continue to shine a light on your path! One thing for sure I know I will never be laid to rest at Arlington National Cemetery.

DISCLAIMER: As I mentioned in my other books -- I wrote this fictional novel in preparation for the creation of a timeless feature film based on this story.

I have been shot at, kidnapped, lost at sea, beaten by a 3rd degree black belt, choked on a chicken bone, got dysentery in the jungle, beaten by a band of monkeys, another words I have outlived my nine lives quite a while ago. Last but not least I survived this wacky chick Stephanie.

However, more recently I died two times in the hospital. I am now recovering from a coma and writing this while still very sick. I decided to slap together this novel of a screenplay. It is loaded with Talking Heads music together as I am a huge Talking Heads fan. Hopefully enough book sale we can actually make this movie.

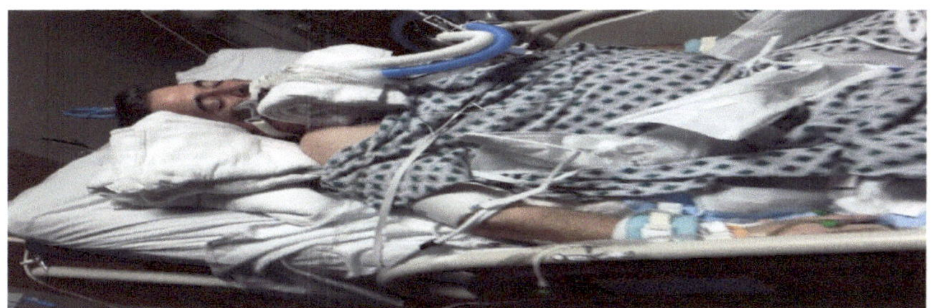

I really hope to live long enough to see this "Novel" of a "Screenplay" shown on the silver screen. There is no "Make A Wish" for someone like me. **Like us on Face Book: Political Illuminati Satire and send us a name of your "bad guy".**

-Daniel A. Shea aka Deaf Bastard aka Mr. 46857

I don’t claim to know Col. Oliver North aka Steel Hammer. I have a great admiration of his “Can Do” spirit. The whole Iran-Contra period was uniquely entertaining for us as the layers were peeled back.

For Ollie I am sure it was an intense and difficult time for him and his family.

CHAPTER ONE

Confidential Informant – A Job So Dangerous No One Wants To Do It

OLIVER NORTH NARRATOR (V.O.) [FROM HEARINGS]

I was <u>authorized</u> to do <u>everything</u> that I <u>did</u>.

I am here to accept responsibility for that which I did.
I will not accept responsibility for that which I did not do.

I want to make it clear that I honestly answered every
question put to me during the so-called Iran-Contra hearings.
But if they didn't ask me about something, I wasn't about to reveal things that
would put other people in jeopardy.

Ask not what you can do for your country but what your country can do for you!!!!

- Oliver North

[Street scene Boston/Brighton Massachusetts midday, clear bright and sunny. People crossing the streets low level of vehicle traffic.]

[Visual: Shea [undercover] picking up drug dealers. 1 woman 2 men. 1 male Latino sits in the passenger seat. Woman and other man sit in the rear of van facing each other. Chatter between rear passengers begins as they open up brief case with powder cocaine.]

[Location: On street across from Farragut
School Boston Mass.]

DAN
Hey Amigo!

[Dan waiving to dealer from the driver side thru the passenger side open window.]

LATINO DEALER
Hey American boy! Are we ready?

[Dealer opens the door and gets in the passenger seat. The others enter thru the sliding door.]

DAN
Yes! Yes lets go!
[van proceeds to move into traffic]

[Undercover DEA Agents begin to follow the van in their car]

LATINO DEALER
[Dealer notices Dan has some device on his ear] American boy what is this thing in your ear?

DAN
(In Spanish) A porquito problema aqiu. Mi no escucha.

DEALER

(TAKES OUT A GUN AND POINTS IT AT DAN'S HEAD)IF YOU ARE A POLICIA I SWEAR I KILL YOU.

DAN
(In Spanish) Mi no polcia. Mi problema in mao cabasa (smiling as the gun in his face doesn't faze him)

DEA AGENT #1
[On the radio] Looks like he is getting ready to move out. Remember stay on him but not to close. There is no way to lose this van with VANISHING POINT mural all over it.Lay low but don't lose em. He drives fast sometimes.

DEA AGENT #2
[On the radio] Copy that's why they gave me this car - to keep up with him if they pull any shenanigans. Last time we lost him - not gonna happen again.

[Out of the blue a 4 wheel drive Chevy Blazer pulls up]

[All vehicles proceed up Commonwealth Avenue toward Brighton Mass.]

DEA AGENT #1
[On the radio] Who the hell is that?

LATINO DEALER
[Dealer notices Dan is looking into is rearview door mirror a lot] Whats the matter American boy?

DAN
Looks like this guy wants to race me.

LATINO DEALER
Gringo it doesn't matter we don't have time for this - lose him!

DAN
Lets see what he has under the hood?

[Dan laughing like a mad man steps on the gas. Latino dealer holds on tight]

[Visual: Picking up speed both Vanishing Point van and Blazer side by side, in and out of traffic]

DEA AGENT # 1
[On the radio] Stay with them - not sure what is going on. HQ run this plate - (mumbling to himself) oh man this is going to blow the whole operation.

[Race continues on Commonwealth Ave towards Brookline. Both van and blazer are driving back and forth over the median strip. Dealers in Vanishing Point are bouncing around in the rear of the van. Cocaine dust everywhere]

[Only to be changed by the sounds ear piercing sound of police sirens as a car chase begins. Racing through the streets near Boston University the police mistakenly interrupts the DEA planned deal.]

[flash to inside van]

[sound of high performance vehicles racing]

[racing attracts attention of local Boston Police - Police cruiser siren and lights go on]

[Now the blue and white Boston Police (BP) cars are chasing the Driver (a HYPED up Chevy Van with Vanishing Point painted on the side)for the DEA transaction. The DEA has to try and cut of the BP cars. In doing so they all accidentally crash.]

[Car chase ends up outside District 14 Police Station. All police cars block. She swerves to miss the police cars and tips Vanishing Point over on the passenger side] [Cartel dealers kick open the rear doors]

[Shoot out ensues]

DEA
DEA
DEA
DEA
DEA
DEA
DEA
DEA

DEA AGENT #1

[Skids to a halt - holding up his badge attempting to get out of his car]

DEA! DEA! DON'T SHOOT!

DEA AGENT #2
[Skids to a halt - holding up his badge also attempting to get out of his car]

[Yelling] DON'T SHOOT EVERYBODY HOLD YOUR FIRE!!

POLICE OFFICER
[TALKING TO DEA AGENT #1]
Did you know him?

DEA AGENT #1
Yes you guys just killed my C1 informant.

[ALL HEADS TURN]

[Another van stops and kind of hysterical guy jumps out dressed in hat and trench coat]

MATT DRUDGE
Hey I know him! I know that guy!! I can't believe it…wow!

POLICE OFFICER
Did you know him? (looking at Shea hanging out the tipped over van - appears to be dead)

MATT DRUDGE
Yes as a matter of fact I do-did. In fact I was asked to proof read a story he was writing. Big coincidence that I happened to be passing by.

POLICE OFFICER
(MATT IS UNAWARE THAT SHEA IS AN INTEL ASSET)
Well what can you tell us about the driver?

MATT DRUDGE BECOMES NARRATOR (V.O.) Well he pretty much began life growing up on Mission Hill in Roxbury Massachusetts. He started out as a surveillance guy working for the DEA and local police

[FLASH TO PAST]
[Fades to Police Detectives at HQ talking to Dan about the risk.]

DEA DETECTIVES [IN THE PAST]
Well YOU are aware that this is a pretty dangerous business with a lot of unpredictable outcomes. You could get killed.

DAN [IN THE PAST]
Look with this thing [pointing to hearing aid in ear] I am already dead. I can't work in any kind of job I want because of this [pointing again]. So I am gonna have fun with this surveillance job and see where it takes me.

[FLASH BACK TO THE PRESENT STORY]

MATT DRUDGE BECOMES NARRATOR (V.O.)
Dan was a bad mother F'er. He would walk into these drug ridden ghettos and slap around some dealers like he was a kingpin… He was a great actor thou….

[FADES TO BLACK]

CHAPTER TWO

THE EARLY YEARS

[DAN'S (AGE 4) MOM ANN IN THE KITCHEN TALKING TO DAN'S 9 YEAR-OLD SISTER)

INT. DAN'S CHILDHOOD HOME - SUNDAY AFTERNOON-DAY

Whats up with the STAR TREK shirts? Family photo

ANN SHEA (MOTHER)
Now remember what I said if you ever have an emergency…
If someone is stuck…
If the house is burning down…
You call 911 (pointing to old rotary phone as Dan is listening in)

[FADE TO BLACK]

[NEXT DAY]

(Dan is trying to get the cookies from the top of the fridge. He can't reach)

DAN (Age 4)
Dad, Dad......

DAN's DAD [sitting in recliner reading the newspaper-not looking up]
What? What is it?

DAN's DAD [sitting in recliner reading the newspaper-not looking up]
Nooooo No cookies until you've had your dinner

DAN[Eyes light up as if lightbulb is turned on]

[Dan reaches for the phone and dials 911] [OLD FASHION ROTARY PHONE]

OPERATOR (911)
911 what is your emergency???

OPERATOR (repeats)
911 what is your emergency???

DANIEL (AGE 4)
Help…. Help.. [holding the phone while trying to reach the cookies - standing on a chair]

<u>EXT. DAN'S CHILDHOOD HOME - SAME DAY-10 MINUTES LATER</u>
[Dan's dad exits the front door with a trash bag in each hand. As he exits he comes to a freeze as the front area is covered with 20 police cars - officers kneeling down with guns drawn]

DAN'S DAD (FROZEN HOLDING TRASH)
Whatz up fellas??

POLICE OFFICER
SOMEONE CALLED 911!!!!

DAN'S DAD (FROZEN HOLDING TRASH BAGS TURNS HIS CHEEK TOWARD THE FRONT DOOR-YELLS)
HONEY THE KIDS ARE PLAYING WITH THE PHONE!!!!

POLICE OFFICER
SOMEONE CALLED 911!!!!
OUT OF THE HOUSE!!!!

[Dan, his sister, his mom and dad are all in the front with their hands up]

DANIEL [Age 4]
Coooooool!!!! [upon seeing all the cops]

MATT DRUDGE BECOMES NARRATOR (V.O.) From that day forward Daniel knew that he wanted to be a policeman or military man and fight crime/war and be a hero…..

JUMP FROM PRESENT TO FLASHBACK

FADE TO: TALKING HEADS (CITIES)
<u>LOCATION: EXT - MISSION GRAMMAR SCHOOL ROXBURY BOSTON MASS</u>

SCENE 1977 Dan is X years-old

[Matt Drudge's voice becomes voice over narrator and the establishing scene is the school yard in Roxbury. The camera pans the black metal gates while kids are playing and the talking heads sound is mixed with kids chatter. The bell rings and recess is over. Kids line up to go back in the school building.]

(Song gets louder) -

Cities"

Think of London, a small city
It's dark, dark in the daytime
The people sleep, sleep in the daytime
If they want to, if they want to

[CHORUS]
I'm checking them out
I'm checking them out
I got it figured out
I got it figured out
There's good points and bad points

[EXT. DAYTIME - CAMSCAN KIDS MISSION GRAMMAR SCHOOL PLAYING IN THE SCHOOL YARD]

[OUR LADY OF PERPETUAL HELP MISSION CHURCH ROXBURY MASSACHUSETTS]

Hey look over there (kids pointing to a stone wall)

SISTER CAROLINA (BOSSY NUN)
Hey you two what do you think you are doing over there!

(Dan and his best friend Nicky (African American boy) are giggling standing side by side. Sister Carolina has a shocked look on her face. The kids lined up are beginning to giggle and laugh. Sister Carolina quickly grabs both the ears of Dan and Nicky.)

SISTER CAROLINA (BOSSY NUN)
What is wrong with you boys? Don't you know this is sacred grounds "LORD HAVE MERCY ON YOU"…..?

SISTER MARY (SWEET NUN)
Oh Sister Carolina! Oh Sister Carolina! What has happened? Why are you holding their ears?

SISTER CAROLINA (BOSSY NUN)
What is wrong? These two decided to practice their cursive and peed their names on the wall during recess.

(Camera flashes to wall where both boys urinated their names on the wall. Dragging the boys away by their ears……)

SISTER MARY (SWEET NUN)

Oh that Daniel is really something. He is going to something wonderful someday. I know it I just know it. Did they at least spell their names correct?

SISTER CAROLINA (BOSSY NUN)

What is wrong with you boys? Don't you know this is sacred grounds "LORD HAVE MERCY ON YOU". You are going to spend the rest of the school year in detention if you keep the malarkey up. I don't have time to deal with you two right now but you better show up for detention, after class. Now go to the Principal's office and tell her what you did. I'll be down in a few minutes.

SISTER MARGARET MARY (THE PRINCIPAL)

Boys I can only imagine why you are in my office.

DAN

Sister Carolina sent us here to tell you the truth, the good, the bad, and the ugly. I am here to tell it all—pleasant and unpleasant, and I am here to accept responsibility for that which I did. I will not accept responsibility for that which I did not do. On that note we plead the 5th as I am also here as a lawyer, "not a potted plant."

NICKY

Aannnd I didn't do anything at all.

DAN

Nicky don't say anything! That is true there is no evidence that we peed on the wall. All we were doing was what Martin Luther King wanted us to do—hang out![Turning to Nicky] Don't worry it's all going to get better in a minute!

32

SISTER MARGARET MARY (THE PRINCIPAL)
Listen - Martin Luther King did have a dream that one day little black boys and little white boys could play together but there was no dream about peeing on the wall!

DAN
Like I said "No comment" and there there is no proof. Okay okay we did pee on the wall. Don't worry Nicky it's all going to get better in a minute.

SISTER MARGARET MARY (THE PRINCIPAL)
Why?

DAN
Okay okay we were practicing cursive. BUT that's our first amendment free speech right- no?

[FADE TO BLACK]

INT. MISSION GRAMMAR SCHOOL CLASSROOM - DAY

[It is all too common for Daniel to be put on the spot which causes panic and anxiety. Being hard of hearing in a group is really difficult for him to hear. He has been ridiculed by the other kids when he cannot answer the Nun's question in front of the class. He has been called names by the other kids(stupid, dumbo, deaf-boy) and others. To counter defend himself he came up with a ventriloquist trick of sort similar Japanese versions of the Godzilla movies actors mouths don't match the words they're saying, and instead of being dubbed over like the movie producers have to do, he's so skilled he can say whatever he wants and have his mouth be shaped completely differently. Dan and his classmates are told to get in groups of six students and the Nun will walk around the room to quiz the group on-the-spot about their studies.]

SISTER CAROLINA (TO CLASS)
Okay class listen up. Today we are going to group together in teams of six. So everybody stand up and spread out 1,2,3, 4, 5, 6 ok you all go over there. Next

group 1,2,3,4,5,6 ---

BAD BOY STUDENT (TO TEAM)
Oh o deaf boy is in our group. Deaf boy look what am I saying (mimicking bad sign language while the other kids are laughing)

[After the Nun has quizzed several groups she aims her sights on Daniel. To catch him off guard because she begins talking with no advance warning. She walks around and her back is to Dan. He cannot see her face and he missed her question and has no idea what she said. He will use this trick throughout his life. He goes into defense mode.]

SISTER CAROLINA (TO CLASS)
So Daniel can you tell me?

DANIEL
[VOICE TRICK)(TO SISTER CAROLINA)

Yes _ did the __ way back at the_____ when there ___ so really it was_______and that was great!

[Dan's mouth is moving but sound is on/off on/off tricking the kids and nun into thinking that it is them not him and that their hearing is screwed up. His ventriloquist mouth movement is really throwing them off. Sister Caroline has put her finger in her ear to see if she can make it hear better. The kids are in disbelief and looking at one another - like huh?]

[She rips off Dan's headphones compares to his friend Nicodemus (Nicky - African American childhood friend/neighbor]

SISTER CAROLINA (TO CLASS)
Children I want you all to meet Father Miller. He is new to the parish. I want you to say our new greeting that we practiced.

STUDENTS
[ALL TOGETHER]
Hello and welcome Father Miller we thank you for being here.

SISTER CAROLINA (TO PRIEST)
This is Daniel he is the one I was telling about. He is my "Special Student".

FATHER MILLER (TO DANIEL)
[TALKING EXTRA LOUD]
HELLO DANIEL. HOW ARE YOU?

(Daniel is looking around from side-to-side to see who the priest was talking to?)

FATHER MILLER (TO DANIEL)
[TALKING EXTRA LOUD]
HELLO DANIEL. HOW ARE YOU? I HEARD YOU ARE HAVING A HARD TIME TO HEAR IN OUR CLASS.

DANIEL
(EXTRA LOUD)
I AM DOING VERY WELL!! THIS IS A NICE PLACE!!! DO YOU HAVE ANY OTHER QUESTIONS???

(Father is taken aback by Dan's loud response Father Miller is a bit stunned and decides to leave the class and get some air.)

SISTER CAROLINA (TO DANIEL)
Daniel why are you always so quiet in my class? Why don't you raise your hand to answer my questions? Why don't you exert yourself and be proactive?

DANIEL
Well I would but listening to you is like watching a Godzilla movie. Your mouth if moving and there is a ten second delay for the sound to catch up. I don't know what you are saying. In a group I don't know who is talking. I don't want to look stupid.

SISTER CAROLINA (TO DANIEL)
Ummmmmm, Ummmmm, Ummmm, Ummmmm, I am going to call your mom to work with her and find a solution.

[Dan can't stand when she says "Ummmmmm" makes him nuts]

DANIEL
Ok fine!

SISTER CAROLINA
(BY TELEPHONE)
Mrs. Shea I am calling you about your son Daniel. He is having a hard time in class to hear. He looks lost so you may need to put him in a school for the deaf or take lip reading class. He will never amount to anything if he doesn't pass my class.

MOTHER (DAN'S MOM)
I am taking you to "Lip Reading" school since you are having a hard time in class.

[Dan and his mother arrive at the Institute for Lip Reading. They enter into a large classroom of more than 30 deaf and hard of hearing students. There are two instructors; the first, an older more scary resemblance of a wicked witch with a mole on her face. The second, a well-endowed blonde Marilyn Monroe look-a-like.]

[THE WITCH LIKE INSTRUCTOR]

GRISELDA

Hello and thank you for coming. My name is Griselda Stitz and I am one of the instructors who will be teaching you lip reading. Lip-reading is an aid to communication for Deaf and hard of hearing people. Lip-reading classes help regain confidence and lessen the feelings of isolation that so often come with hearing loss. Most people misunderstand deafness.
It's invisible and doesn't change the way you appear to other people, but it can change the way you feel. You may feel excluded from everyday activities and conversations, find it difficult to cope in some situations, feel frustrated when trying to communicate with people around you. I want you to know that I know deafness undermines confidence and independence and the effects permeate all aspects of a person's life. And now I would like to introduce our newest instructor Miss Anna Nicole.

[The young woman marches at a moderate speed toward the camera, and passes Dan and his mom with all her well endowdness and steps up to the front of the class.]

THE 2ND INSTRUCTOR (ANNA NICOLE)

Hello and welcome. In just a moment we will divide the class into two groups by last names. If your name ends with the letter A thru P you will be in my group. P thru Z you will be in Griselda's class.

DAN (TO HIS MOM)

Mom our name ends with "S" …there is no way I can be in Griselda's class.

DAN'S MOM (TO DAN)
Why not? Why can't you be in her class?

DAN
Griselda look too much like Sister Carolina. She is the nun I cannot get along with. There is no way I can read her lips. I need to be in Ms. Nicole's class. I promise I will really really read her lips well.

DAN'S MOM (TO DAN)
Okay okay I'll make a special request to have you in Ms. Nicole's class.

(Dan's mother walks down the hallway to Ms. Nicole's office to ask her if she would take on Dan.)

DAN'S MOM (TO MS. NICOLE)
Ms. Nicole could I ask you a favor?

MS. NICOLE
Yes, what is it?

DAN'S MOM (TO MS. NICOLE)
Would you mind if my son Daniel attends your class vise Ms. Griselda? It is a personality thing - she reminds him too much of the Catholic Nun at his school.

MS. NICOLE
Okay I guess. Just show up at the class in the Boston Public Library after school on Monday for his hearing and sign language assessment.

DAN'S MOM (TO MS. NICOLE)
Okay we will see you there.

EXT. BOSTON PUBLIC LIBRARY --- DAY
(Dan and his mom arrive outside the door of Ms. Nicole's rented classroom space for lip-reading and sign language. In the waiting room there is another boy a little bit older than Dan.)

DAN'S MOM (TO DAN)
Okay we they call your name go into the room. I am going to look for some books so stay right here until I get back.

BENNY (TO DANIEL)
Hi my name is Benny is this your first day?

DANIEL
Hi my name is Daniel - yes this is my first day here. Are you in Ms. Nicole's class?

BENNY (TO DANIEL)
Yes I am. If it is your first day then Ms. Nicole is going to give you a test on your sign and lip reading skills. Do you want me to teach you 3 easy signs?

DANIEL
ok

BENNY (TO DANIEL)
Ok the first one is how to say "yes" using sign. (makes a Y with fingers) and the second is how you say "no" sticks up his middle finger. And the 3rd is how you make a girl smile (a V while licking with tongue).

MS. NICOLE (TO DANIEL)
Hi Daniel please step into my office. Please have a seat. Today I want to find out how much you can hear and understand. What do you already know about sign language and lip reading?

DANIEL
Well I know some sign language.

MS. NICOLE
Oh that's great. Go ahead and show me.

DANIEL
Oh this is how to say "yes" and this is how you say "no" (middle finger) and this is how to make a……….

MS. NICOLE
Nooooo!! Don't do it!!!!!

MS. NICOLE
Oh I see you have met Benjamin!!

[Dan finishes his first 3 weeks he is beginning to read peoples lips everywhere. It's becoming a problem because he now hears voices with his eyes. He can eavesdrop on anyone near or far away. He wanders around the library and realizes all the books are like a treasure of information. He begins to flip through several. He notices the signs with each reading section. He heads to the library lobby where a homeless man is sitting on the floor. At first Dan doesn't even notice him when Dan is thinking out loud and shouts - "I have arrived!!!!"

[BOSTON PUBLIC LIBRARY]

HOMELESS GUY (TO DANIEL)

Oh yes you have arrive!! I take it you just discovered the treasure trove of information in the library?

DANIEL

Yes that's right how did you know?

HOMELESS GUY (TO DANIEL)

I well kid when you have been around as long as I have you see a few things learn a few things and then you figure - hey I don't have to wait for the teacher I can figure out a solution for the problem myself. Low and behold all the solutions are here in the library waiting to be discovered by a young lad like you. But don't you forget - you can do it all! The world is yours….

We have science here! World issues, biographies, read all about people from other lands - then go there and kill them. (that comment put a surprised smirk on Daniel's face) And kid don't forget to visit the secret military room. It closed off to the public. Has all kinds of goodies that they forgot to redact. The world is yours so go out and make something of yourself!

DANIEL

That's right I don't have to wait! I can read all day! Every day!and figure it all out myself. And just how old are you?

HOMELESS GUY (TO DANIEL) Thirty-five. (Looks like 85)

DANIEL

Well what happened to you? Why are you here living in the library and not living your dream?

HOMELESS GUY (TO DANIEL)

My glasses broke and I just gave up.

DANIEL

Don't you worry - everything is gonna get better in a minute.

[FADE TO BLACK]

EXT. BOSTON PUBLIC LIBRARY --- DAY

(Dan is sorting a stack of books from his table in the Boston Public Library he comes across "The Secrets of Coral Castle - how to move objects easily" Dan places the book in the middle of the table and begins to read page after page.)

INT. OLPH CLASSROOM --- DAY

SISTER CAROLINA (BOSSY NUN)

Don't forget Daniel and Bruce you have make up detention after class today. I want both you to show up at the Nuns convent just across the way. You are going to mop up our floors so they are SPIC and SPAN.

INT. CONVENT --- DAY

NICKY

I don't know Dan. I don't know this place looks spooky.

[Entering the very large front doors Dan and Nic enter into the very large living room area where there are several elderly nuns scatter around sleeping on various sofas. Carrying their mops they continue to walk around looking up at the cathedral ceiling with many statues. Starring at the sleeping nuns)

NICKY

Are they dead? I can swear this one ain't breathing.

DAN
I think your right.

[Very loud and noisy Sister Carolina makes her way into the room. When she speaks with her booming voice it echoes throughout the convent. Regardless none of the sleeping elderly nuns even twitch nor move. Still sound asleep.

SISTER CAROLINA (BOSSY NUN)
Okay boys grab your mops and buckets. I want this place SPIC and SPAN BY THE TIME I GET BACK! Is that clear? And no hanky panky!!

DAN & NICKY (TOGETHER)
Yes Sister Carolina - SPIC and SPAN.
[Sister Carolina picks up her brief case and bag and goes out the front door. The boys begin to mumble and grumble mimicking the bossy Nun. Okay boys grab your mops and buckets.]

NICKY
I thought SPIC and SPAN was a bad word?

DAN
I think SPIC is the bad word. I don't think SPAN is.

About two hours later Sister Carolina returns with a flock of nuns. She opens the door and yells to the boys.

SISTER CAROLINA (BOSSY NUN)
Okay boys put away your mops and buckets you are free to go. I hope you have learned your lesson.
[The boys put away their mop and buckets in the closet and as they are scrambling to get out they pass Sister Mary and the other nuns just arriving.]

SISTER MARY (SWEET NUN)
That Daniel! Oh he is really going to be something when he grows up!
NUN SUSPENDED UP NEAR CEILING ON THE WAGON WHEEL CHANDELIER
EEEEEKKKKKKKKKKKKKKKKKKKKKKKK!!!!!

SISTER CAROLINA (BOSSY NUN)
OH MY GOD! WHAT ARE YOU DOING UP THERE?
NUNS ARE SUSPENDED UP NEAR CEILING

I don't know I just fell asleep on the sofa- who did this to us???

SISTER CAROLINA (BOSSY NUN)

[Laughing to herself] Hang on sisters we'll get you down…….

EXT. CONVENT --- EVE

As the boys run out the front door you hear Sister Carolina shriek. Sister Carolina has discovered all the elderly nuns that were sleeping on the sofas in the room the boys were moping are now suspended high up using the wagon wheel chandeliers over the living room (still sleeping). The boys had utilized the Secrets of Coral Castle technology to hoist up the sleeping nuns 25 feet up.

[FADE TO BLACK]

CHAPTER THREE

WAR GAMES

EXT. SOUTH WHITNEY STREET BOSTON -- ESTABLISHING - DAY

(A very large six family house was sold to Mr. Finch. He is just pulling up the sold sigh and handing it back to the real estate agent. Dan and his friends always played street soccer, hockey and other games out front of Mr. Finch newly acquired home.)

MR. FINCH (TO THE KIDS PLAYING ON THE STREET)

Okay! Okay! Kids listen up! There wil be no more ball playing on this street! If I see any one of you playing out here I will call the police! Do I make myself clear?

Kids shaking their heads with a tear in their eyes.

[Mr. Finch kicks us off S. Whitney Street - no more soccer]

DAN (TO KIDS ON THE STREET)
Okay guys you know what this means??? This means WAR!!

KIDS ON THE STREET (TOGETHER)
YEAH!!!! Okay okay whattddya we do?

DAN (TO KIDS ON THE STREET)
Okay first we gotta know everything thing about this enemy. We have to do surveillance.

KIDS ON THE STREET (TOGETHER)
Surveillance? What's that??

DAN (TO KIDS ON THE STREET)
Butchy, Barry, Babe you guys follow me. Stephen and Jay keep an eye out for the enemy and let us know what he does when we get back.

BABE (TO KIDS ON THE STREET)

Where are we going guys I have to be home by five.

DAN (TO BUTCHY, BARRY AND BABE)
Guys we are going to stock up on our supplies. We are going to visit the Red Cross building on Tremont Street.

EXT. RED CROSS BUILDING --- EVE (As the boys hang around out front a delivery driver shows up and gets buzzed in to the lobby of Red Cross.)

DAN (TO BUTCHY, BARRY AND BABE)
Okay guys inside that front door is a freezer that holds ice. All I need to do is get a couple of those bags to a make our secret weapon. On my que I will get inside and throw out a bag to each of you.
The next delivery guy shows up and Dan stands silently behind him. Once the driver is buzzed in Dan sneaks right in behind him. Dan makes his way to the freezer under the stair case and opens the door. He grabs each bag that is steaming with smoke. He opens the front door and gives a bag to each of his friends.

BABE (TO KIDS ON THE STREET)
Look its smoking ----why is it smoking?

DAN (TO KIDS ON THE STREET)

This is called dry ice. It is not the same as regular ice. In fact you cannot touch it with your fingers - they will fall off.

BABE (TO KIDS ON THE STREET)
Okay cool now what????

DAN (TO KIDS ON THE STREET)
Follow me……………….

EXT. SATURDAY AFTERNOON ON TOP OF MISSION HILL MOUNTIAN OVERLOOKING SOUTH WITHNEY STREET. --- DAY

(The boys are all dressed in Army play clothes, hat, BDUs, boots etc. On the very top they are all inside a bunker dug out of the dirt. The scenery is of a hot arid dessert.)

DAN (TO NICKY) [FLUTE MUSIC HIGH NOON]
Do you see the enemy?

NICKY (TO DAN)
No sir, nothing but dust?

DAN (TO NICKY AND GROUP)
Do you think we should launch our attack and defeat the enemy? I think it's the right time of day. We have the upper advantage as the sun sets it will blind the eyes of the enemy. Most people think that the sun is directly overhead at noon. The truth is that this rarely happens. As a matter of fact, there are many places where this never happens (like Waukesha, Wisconsin). So where exactly is the sun in the sky? If you've never thought about it, you probably have never noticed. Today the sun is right where we want it right guys????
ALL SHAKING THEIR HEADS YES IN SYNCH WITH EACH OTHER

DAN (TO STEPHEN AND GROUP)
Ok you guys take your gear and lets move out…..

(One by one they crawl out of the dusty bunker hole in the ground. Dragging knap sacks and other gear the get up and run toward the edge of the cliff that overlooks South Whitney Street. Peeking over the edge with the sun rays behind them the kids are taking a risk looking down. From the ground up view you just see the glare of the sun.)
(Mr. Finch is doing what he does every Saturday morning - washes his car using a bucket of water. Wearing his black frame bifocals and white tank top t-shirt, dress trousers and shoes he sits on a milk crate with a sponge in hand to work on his car wheels.)
(The kids are preparing six two liter bottles by tying them to ropes to lower them down next to the unsuspecting enemy - Mr. Finch)

DAN (WHISPERING TO GROUP)
Ok guys fill these balloons with baby powder and them tie them to the bottle.

STEPHEN (WHISPERING TO GROUP)
Yeah baby powder for the cry baby. But how much water do we add to the bottle.

DAN (WHISPERING TO GROUP)
You fill it almost to the top - shove in 2 cubes of dry ice. Close it tight - shake to activate timer then lower.

DAN (WHISPERING TO GROUP)

10, 9, 8, 7, 6, 5, 4, 3, 2

[By now Mr. Finch is hand waxing his beautiful car. Behind him from above are the six two liter bottles full of food coloring, dry ice, and a balloon with baby powder for special effects.
(BOOM!! BOOM!! BOOM!! BOOM!! BOOM!! BOOM!! The sound is deafening. Car alarms are going off. The color water sprayed everywhere. A blinding dust ball from the baby powder is rising up in the air. Mr. Finch's glasses are crooked on his face. He and his car are painted red, yellow and green. Yelling at the top of his lung raising his fist to the sky……)

MR. FINCH (SQUINTING HIS EYES- SENSES SOMETHING)
YOU LITTLE BASTARDS!!!! I AM GOING TO GET YOU!!! I AM GOING TO GET YOU!!! Finch jumps I his car and drives to the top of the Mission Hill mountain. He drives his car as close as it will go before getting stuck. He jumps out shaking his fist at the kids off in a short distance.

(Song fades in)

***TALKING HEADS* Burning Down The House Lyrics**

Watch out you might get what you're after
Boom babies strange but not a stranger
I'm an ordinary guy
Burning down the house

Hold tight wait till the party's over
Hold tight We're in for nasty weather
There has got to be a way
Burning down the house

Here's your ticket pack your bag: time for jumpin' overboard
The transportation is here
Close enough but not too far,
Maybe you know where you are..

(The kids scramble to get to the other side of the cliff and climb down to Dan's back yard of his parents 3 decker apartment building. Once down in Dan's yard the kids begin to climb up the back porch drain pipe - all the way up to the roof of the 3 story building. They can still hear Finch yelling at a short distance)

[BACK PORCH OF DAN'S HOUSE WHERE WE CLIMBED UP TO THE ROOF AND JUMPED OVER TO THE NEXT BUILDING WHEN FINCH CHASED US]

(F
inch also climbs down to Dan's back yard. He looks up and see the foot of the last kid make his way onto the roof. All the kids huddle up behind chimney scared. It is a bright blue sunny sky. The sun is shining down on them and their shadow is shown on the roof and chimney.)

DAN (WHISPERING TO GROUP)
Okay everybody pray, pray, get down on your knees and pray!

KID (TO THE GROUP)
If I am going pray I am going to pray for x-ray vision!

DAN (LEADING THE GROUP)
This guy is going to kill us you better pray he doesn't. Our father who art in heaven…..

STEPHEN (TO THE GROUP)
Hey! Hey! I am not even Christian!

(Dan looking around for water finds a soup can over on the corner of the roof filled with rain water - he runs over to it. Picks it up and runs back to group behind the chimney. Nervously he dips three fingers in the can and begins baptizing each kid by splashing the water on to their heads….. Mr. Finch now on the third floor porch is still climbing to the top of the roof.)

DAN (TO THE GROUP)
I now baptize you in the name Father, Son and Holy Spirit. I now baptize you in the name of Father, Son and Holy Spirit. What??? The water works the same for everyone….Don't worry everything is going to get better in a minute…

(All eyes to the drainpipe area of the roof] - [Song fades and theme from JAWS tunes in -beat beat)
(The kids are back on their knees - nervously praying, eyes closed)
(Mr. Finch is yelling and here comes his arm reaching over the drain pipe trying to grab onto something to pull himself up on to the roof.)

CRACK!!! SNAP!!!
[Mr. Finch face is frozen. The drainpipe has cracked and about to fall.]

MR. FINCH (FALLING)
AAAAAAAAAAAAAAAAHHHHHHHHHHHHHHHHHH HHHHHHH!!!!!!!!!!!!!!!!!!!!!!

The kids open their eyes and look at each other with joy on their face.

DAN (TO THE GROUP)
Guys…You've been saved.

STEPHEN (TO DAN)
Dan are you going to be a priest when you grow up?

DAN (TO STEPHEN)
No for sure. My Dad was a Marine, My uncle was a Marine. I am going to be a Marine - gonna kick azzz HOO HAA ---FOLLOW ME!

(All the kids follow Dan by jumping from one roof to the next (3 stories high). Camera view from alley upward to see as the jump over to the next house. Fade to black.)

NARRATOR VO

(At age eleven - to improve his confidence Dan's mom registered him in the local Roxbury Karate Academy. After months of training Dan is ready to compete. On this particular day Dan's dad cannot pick them up from the tournament. Dan's uncle and cousins are coming to watch the karate show and then drive Dan and his mom home.

INT. KARATE MATCH RING SIDE - [NOISY ROOM IS PACKED WITH PARENTS AND KIDS WAITING FOR THE KARATE MATCH TO BEGIN] FLASH FORWARD TO 1ST MATCH, FLASH 2ND MATCH AND FINALLY DAN'S TURN TO COMPETE]

RINGSIDE KARATE ANNOUNCER
To my left of the ring is mighty Mike an alltime favorite of Mission Hill and to my right is deaf boy - I mean Danny Boy also from Mission Hill and quite an egotistical maniac.

DANIEL (WHISPERING TO HIS COACH)
Did he just call me a testical?

[DAN'S MOM, UNCLE AND TWO COUSINS 7 AND 9 YEARS OLD ENTERING THE EVENT ROOM.]

DAN'S MOM (TALKING LOUD)[FACING EVENT]
Yes I signed Dan up for this academy - I don't know if you are aware but kids like Dan - with his hearing loss and all develop extra special perception.

DAN'S UNCLE (TALKING LOUD)[FACING EVENT]
You mean ESP? Extrasensory perception or ESP, also called sixth sense, includes reception of information not gained through the recognized physical senses but sensed with the mind.

DAN'S MOM (TALKING LOUD)
Yaaaa that's it. I watched him when he was younger - ohhh Dan's up next

[Dan and his much larger opponent enter the ring and the bell rings]

MIGHTY MIKE [FAKE SIGN LANGUAGE]
What am I saying deaf boy?
Ami saying something? Huh huh(jumping around the ring)

DAN [IN ONE SWIFT MOVE-GRABS MIKE'S FINGER](SINGING ALOUD)
WHAT DID THE FOX SAY?? HE SAID OWWWUCH! (MIMICKING MIKE'S PAIN)

MIGHTY MIKE [IN PAIN]
OOOOOOwwwww you DEAF BASTARD!!

RINGSIDE KARATE ANNOUNCER
And there off!! Uppercut, mid block reverse by Shea! Low block -what that was 5 punches by Mighty Mike! Bam! Boom! Bam! Look at that deaf monkey go!!
Shea comes back with Double Knife hands and a kick to Mike's head! Open hand

throat strike by Shea and Mighty Mike is down for the count!! Gasping for air..

DAN'S UNCLE (TALKING LOUD)[BEGINS TO WALK AWAY FROM THE EVENT-VISUALLY SEE DAN AND MIKE OVER UNCLE'S SHOULDER]
Wow look at that I had no idea he was that good…

DAN'S MOM (TALKING LOUD)[EVENT IN BACKGROUND-WALKING AWAY TALKING]
Ya as I was saying ESP. I saw him running and jumping over mail boxes [flash to Dan on street running and jumping over things]
He even jumped over a parked car.

[GETTING INTO UNCLE'S STATION WAGON]

(UNBEKNOWNEST TO DAN'S MOM, UNCLE AND TWO COUSINS MIGHTY MIKES REBOUNDS AND GET UP AND CHOPS DAN IN THE GUT, NECK AND-DAN MEETS THEM OUTSIDE AND GETS IN THE BACK SEAT OF A STATION WAGON WITH A COUSIN ON EACH SIDE. HIS MOM AND UNCLE IN THE FRONT SEAT TALKING AWAY AND JUST THEN DAN HAS THE NEED TO VOMIT.

DAN'S COUSINS NOTICE HIS VOMIT EXPRESSION ON HIS FACE AS HE PLACES TWO FINGERS OVER HIS MOUTH. DAN TURNS HIS HEAD TO THE LEFT AND HIS COUSIN (SCARED)SHAKES HIS HEAD NO- AND POINTS TO THE OTHER COUSIN. THAT COUSIN ALSO (SCARED) SHAKES HER HEAD NO AND POINTS TO BROTHER. DAN CAN'T DECIDE WHERE TO THROW UP AS THE PARENT'S ARE TALKING ABOUT ESP AND CAR IS DRIVING - DAN PULLS OUT A COIN AND FLIPS HEADS/OR TAILS BUT CAN'T WAIT….)

DAN (VOMITING IN THE CAR BACKSEAT FROM THE KARATE CHOPS)
AAAAAAAARRRRRRRRGGGGGGGGG -

(SCREEN GOES BLACK)

DAN
SORRY!!

<u>EXT. TOBIN GYM --- DAY</u>

NARRATOR V.O.
13 year old young Dan is just minding his own business when three older white kids confront him on the basketball court. They ridicule him calling him deaf boy and retard. Unbeknownst to Dan his African-American friend Nicky is at the other end of the court with his friends - twelve of them.

TROUBLE MAKER 1
Hey deaf boy!! Yeah you! I'm talking to you. Why did you take my ball?

TROUBLE MAKER 2
Yeah! Why did you take his ball? Guys I forgot (using his fingers to mimick sign language). You deaf bastard! Can you hear me now?

DAN
Guys really now I don't want any trouble.

I __ really ____ you know_____

TROUBLE MAKER 3
Do you see what he did? He is messing with you. His mouth is moving but he isn't saying anything.
[The trouble maker is getting ready to strike Dan with his fist]

DAN
Guys really ___ I don't want ___trouble _____

NICKY (TO HIS ENTOURAGE)
Hey guys FOLLOW me.

[Nicky and is group of 12 run down the court towards Dan and grab the 3 troublemakers. Holding their arms behind their backs taunting Dan to take a swing at them]

NICKY'S ENTOURAGE (CHANTING IN SYNC)
Hit em! Hit em! HIT THEM DAN!!!!

DAN (USING A HILLBILLY REDNECK ACCENT)
Iffin youd be more spific bout what your askin I might be able to help youins out.

NICKY
Dan meanness don't happen overnight. These guys are slower than molasses in January but they are mean.

DAN
(USING A HILLBILLY REDNECK ACCENT)Welllllllll looki here. Looks like we got us a couple good fur nothing trouble makers up here. This one is sweating like a whore in church and balder than a peeled egg. Nicky your right I feel like I've been shot at and missed. Shit at and hit!

NICKY
(USING A HILLBILLY REDNECK ACCENT)
You got that right!

DAN
(USING A HILLBILLY REDNECK ACCENT)
These three are not the brightest bulbs in the box.

NICKY
(USING A HILLBILLY REDNECK ACCENT)
Not the sharpest knife in the drawer.

DAN
(USING A HILLBILLY REDNECK ACCENT)
The lights are on but nobody is home!

NICKY
(USING A HILLBILLY REDNECK ACCENT)
The engine is running but nobody is driving!

DAN
(USING A HILLBILLY REDNECK ACCENT)
They are so dumb they could throw themselves on the ground and miss!

NICKY
(USING A HILLBILLY REDNECK ACCENT)
Three sandwiches shy of a picnic!

DAN
(USING A HILLBILLY REDNECK ACCENT)
Three fries short of a happy meal! Nicky I rekon these boys are racist!!

TROUBLE MAKERS
(AT THE SAME TIME)
No way! No sir! We are not racist.

DAN
(STARING AT THE 3 TROUBLEMAKERS)Oh yea! If you guys are not racist then kiss the cheerleaders.

[Most beautiful black cheerleader appears and leans on Dan's shoulder. Dan and the cheerleader kiss and nibble a bit]

TROUBLE MAKERS (AT THE SAME TIME)
Okay okay alright-we will do it. We'll kiss the cheerleader.

[Walking over are three overweight, one eyebrow, scary teeth, hard-to-look-at black female cheerleaders]

[The three troublemakers turn into the three stooges (imitating Curly)

TROUBLE MAKERS
(AT THE SAME TIME)
Aye, yi,yi, whob, whob,whob…….my gosh! I just don't know. Can't we all just get along?

[Three more of Nicky's friends come over with blankets and ropes.]

DAN
(USING VENTROLQUISM TRICK)
DEAF BASTARD!!

NICKY
(USING A HILLBILLY REDNECK ACCENT)
Well I'll be (staring at the 3

troublemakers-about to punch their lights out)

DAN
Nicky, Nicky don't do it! (standing between Nicky and troublemakers)

DAN
(AGAIN USING VENTROLQUISM TRICK)
DEAF BASTARD!!

[NICKY HOLDING DAN BACK]

TROUBLE MAKER 2
What? It wasn't me I didn't even say anything!

DAN
[DROPS THE HILLBILLY ACCENT AND BEGINS RANT] Do have any idea why I don't talk in class?

TROUBLE MAKER 2
No idea.

DAN
What?

TROUBLE MAKER 2
No idea. (all are staring at Dan)

DAN
I don't talk because I can't hear! I am afraid I can't hear so I don't want anyone to ask me anything just so I don't look stupid!!

Do you know I was almost killed in a thunderstorm by siding that was blown off a house because I couldn't hear it coming!!!

Do you know that I got hit by a car while running across the street because I couldn't hear it coming?

Do you know that my very first girlfriend DIED!!!

TROUBLE MAKER 2
Because you couldn't hear her coming? (all chuckling)

NICKY
(NO ACCENT)
She died?

DAN
NO she almost died!!!!
Because she inhaled.

TROUBLE MAKER 2
She inhaled?

DAN
Yes! We were kissing and necking and she inhaled my hearing aid - I didn't know so I kept kissing her and before ya know wit she huffing and puffing and gagging and I just thought maybe I had bad breath and then it dawned on me that I couldn't hear anything. She damn near choked to death. Do you see what I am saying? Do ya! Do ya!

DAN
(USING A HILLBILLY REDNECK ACCENT)
OK YOU THREE - KISSE'EM OR GO TO THE FOUNTAINS!!

THE FUGLIEST CHEERLEADER
I WANT THAT ONE (POINTING TO TROUBLEMAKER 3)

Nicky I'd be happier than a tornado in a trailer park if you'd take these three over to the fountain. *TO THE FOUNTAIN!!*

TROUBLE MAKER 2
Whaddya mean to the fountain? [Looking at the scary cheerleaders] I can't do it!

DAN (STARING AT THE 3 TROUBLEMAKERS)
A word of advice - Don't mess with a deaf guy -- be careful you don't corner something meaner than you. And watch out as the meek are going to inherit the earth.

DAN (USING A HILLBILLY REDNECK ACCENT)
I say! TO THE FOUNTAIN!!

[Nicky's friends (6ft tall) tie up the 3 trouble makers and wrap them in red large blankets and carry them across the basketball court then outside to the school fountain singing 'Camptown Ladies" very loud as a group. The gym is filling up as there is about to be a game starting]

Camptown ladies sing this song, do-da, do-da,
Camptown racetrack's two miles long, oh, the do-da day.
Goin' to run all night, goin' to run all day,
I bet my money on a bob-tailed nag,

somebody bet on the gray.
The long-tailed filly and the big black horse, do-da, do-da,
Come to the mud hole and they all cut across, oh, the do-da day.
Goin' to run all night, goin' to run all day,
I bet my money on a bob-tailed nag,
somebody bet on the gray I went down South with my hat caved in, do-da, do-da,
I came back North with a pocket full of tin, oh, the do-da day.
Goin' to run all night, goin' to run all day,
I bet my money on a bob-tailed nag,
somebody bet on the gray

DAN (To the audience with his hands in the air)
WHATS MY NAME!!!!x3 [points to the north, points to the south, points up]

THE AUDIENCE (ROAR - SHOUTS BACK)
DEAF BASTARD!!!!!!!x3

(The three trouble makers are tied to the TOP of school fountain in just their underwear. A tennis ball tied over their mouths and standing up the water spout is between their legs. It appears that they are peeing every time the water turns on. The entire girl soccer team is giggling as they pass by.)
The sign on the water fountain kids ------reads:
DEAF BASTARD WAS HERE!!!

CHAPTER FOUR

TEENAGE VANISHING POINT

(FLASH FORWARD > Dan is now 15 years old but looks older like 21.)

DAN (TO USED CAR SALESMAN)
Does it run well?

USED CAR SALESMAN
Does it run well? Well of course it runs well!

DAN
Why is that yellow light on - check engine?

USED CAR SALESMAN
Oh that light. Think of it like this. You about to fly and airplane and your copilot says " radio" you say check, "pressure" and you say check!, engine and you check! Get it "engine" check that's all that is……

DAN
(TO BABE WHILEWALKING AWAY FROM DEALER)
He thinks I was born on a Tuesday when in fact I was not!!

<u>EXT. FRONT OF DAN'S HOUSE (STREET --- DAY</u>

DAN'S DAD

Dan now that you have your driver's license I have a surprise for you.

DAN
Oh really what can it be?

DAN'S DAD
I won this van during a card game the other night. I want you to have it under one condition. No speeding, no racing, no groups of kids driving around goofing off with you. You got it?

Vanishing Point

DAN
That is 3 conditions - ok just kidding!
THIS IS SO GREAT!! What is on the side?
Says "Vanishing Point"………

DAN'S DAD
So do we have a deal?

DAN
DEAL!!!

(DAN MEETS A FRIEND OF BABE A POLICE OFFICE NAMED GEORGE. GEORGE a local Boston police officer assigned to the DEA task force, who quickly realized that Dan's lip reading skill makes him an ideal candidate to become a member of a surveillance task force. Since the inception of cell telephones coming on the market law enforcement could not tap the cell phones so easy. Dan agreed to become a surveillance team member as a lip reader without a clear idea of what that meant and how dangerous it was. A good lip reader with high powered binoculars or in the rear view mirror of a car could read the dealer's lips to gain crucial real time intel. Dan just wanted to drive fast and get out of speeding tickets for fun>)

(Officer George puts Dan through a test. Both George and a senior detective at West Roxbury HQ)

SENIOR DETECTIVE (EXPLAINING TO GEORGE)
Not only do many words look similar, letters formed mostly with the tongue look identical. Look in the mirror, sometime, and say the letters t, c, g and z, and try to tell which one is which. You can't. Now, imagine security droids looking at what the computer thinks somebody is saying and taking it as the literal truth because, as we all know, computers never lie. Be afraid. Be very afraid.

However, this ability is greatly overstated in fiction where the deaf are concerned, since it's fairly difficult to master and not all deaf people can do it, and even those that can are never perfect. In English, less than half of spoken sounds can be seen on the lips; the rest rely on the throat and tongue movements. That's how we get the joke about how **"olive juice"** looks exactly like **"I love you."**

I know, from research and real-world experience with people with intensive speech-reading training, that lipreading will yield, at most, about 25% of speech. There are simply too many words that look alike or resist analysis to grasp more than that. You can fill in some of the blanks by the situational context, body language and residual hearing, if there is any. But frankly I see this as an effort to take advantage of gullible government agencies by touting a gee-whiz technological solution that won't work. SOOOOO -- WE MUST USE THE DEAF BASTARD!!!

SENIOR DETECTIVE (VISUALLY TESTING DAN)
atwhay teh uckfay you alkingtay aboutay?

LEARNING LAW BEGINS********

<u>EXT. ROLINDALE MASS (STREET) (DUNKIN DOUGHNUTS) --- DAY</u>
[Dan and his friend are sitting at a RED LIGHT on Washington Street Roslindale Mass in his van.]

[There is a small dog in the passenger seat all dressed up with a coat and hat in the pickup truck next to Dan's van. Dan begins to taunt the dog without the dog's owner/driver being able to see what's going on. Dan puts on funny bulging eyeglasses and vampire teeth. The dog starts going nuts… Dan and Nicky are laughing it up.]

NICKY

Did you see that dog all dressed up - that's insane!

DAN

I heard that owner that do that must attend sensitivity training since the dogs begin to lose their identity. They think they are human.

[As traffic slowly moves forward]

[Dan begins looking in his rearview mirror sees a beautiful well-endowed girl.]

[Stephanie in her dark blue mercury marquis car tan roof with her girlfriend Debbie.]

[Dan hits his friend on the shoulder and signals him to look out his driver side window toward Stephanie's car. Stephanie and her girlfriend doesn't even notice the van next to her car.]

[Both Dan and his friend still gawking staring at the two hotties. Just then Stephanie begins looking in her car mirror - contemplating picking her nose.]

DAN

Nicky what's bigger watermelons or coconuts?

NICKY

WATERMELONS FOR SURE!!!!

DAN

Nicky get ready to see some of the best watermelons, coconuts, bAzingazzzzz of your life!!
[Nick and Dan high fiving]

NICKY

GODZILLAS! cantaloupes, chumbawumbas, BAZINGAZZZZ!!!! I am so happy we are not all created alike! I would hate to see the same size breast on every woman.

DAN

Yeah bazingazzz……….. [using the finger to show erection] LOL Godzillas really? I have never heard that one.

[Dan and Nick are watching Stephanie about to pick her nose]

DAN AND NICKY [TOGETHER]

………Nooooo Noooo don't do it!

NICKY

EEEEEwwwwwwwwww!!! Did you see that? Yuck Yuck. Oh that's so disgusting!

DAN

Yea but they still look good thou.

DAN'S PASSENGER

Okay you can have the driver - just don't let feed you by hand [LOL]

DAN

(YELLING OUT THE CAR WIDOW)Hey baby! Hey baby! Do you need help with that construction project?

DEBBIE (TO STEPHANIE)

Whose that guy? Do you know him? What construction project is he talking about?

STEPHANIE (TO DEB)

Okay I am going to pull over at Dunkin Doughnuts to see what he wants. He is kinda cute.

DEBBIE (TO STEPHANIE)

No no lets keep going! Forget about them! Com'on I don't want to meet them.

STEPHANIE (TO DEB)

Oh just for a minute. At least let me get his phone number. Think about it he might pay for my gas. You never know.

[They all park in the Dunkin Doughnuts parking lot in Rossi Square. Dan and his friend exits his Vanishing Point van. Stephanie and Debbie step out of Stephanie's car.]

STEPHANIE (TO DAN)

Hi how are you. My name is Stephanie and this is my girlfriend Debbie.

DAN (TO STEPHANIE)

Hi how are you. My name is Dan and this is Nicky. Nice to meet you.

DEBBIE (TO DAN)

Hi how are you what are you guys up to? And what construction are you talking about?

DAN (TO DEB)

Do you really want to know? Really? While you were looking out your window at us you frind over there was digging for gold (mimicking drilling her nostril)

DEBBIE (TO STEPHANIE)
Ewwww did you do that? That's gross!

[The night goes later and later. The van music is on Dan and Steph begin making out. Kissing and moving about in the van with the sliding door open. Out of the blue Dan's other friends (Nicky, Babe, Gerard, Joey Bale, John Sullivan, Barry, Butchie, Mike Viola, Frankie, x, x)show up and discovered Dan and Stephanie are hooked. All Dan's friends are standing at the van door gawking.]

BABE (TO DAN)
Ahem! Ahem! Dan can I talk to you for a minute?

DAN (TO HIS FRIENDS)
Hey guys! I didn't see you standing there. Did you see what kinda fish I caught today? Come on everyone jump in and lets go for a ride.

CAMERA TOURS THE CITY OF BOSTON DOWNTOWN, NORTHEND, BROOKLINE, MISSION HILL, ROSLINDALE, ETC.

Sound fades in Talking Heads - City of Dreams Lyrics

Here where you are standing, dinosaurs did a dance
The Indians told a story, now it has come to pass
The Indians had a legend, the Spaniards lived for gold
The white man came and killed them but they haven't really gone

We live in the city of dreams
We drive on this highway of fire
Should we awake and find it gone
Remember this, our favorite town

EXT. DOWNTOWN BOSTON (STREET) (COMBAT ZONE) --- NIGHT
[Driving thru Boston's red light combat zone Dan is pulled over for having too many kids in his van.]

POLICE OFFICER (TO DAN)

Step out of the car son. Do you know why I am pulling you over?

DAN

No sir. I don't drink, smoke, didn't run any red lights. I think I am doing okay. So what did I do?

POLICE OFFICER (TO DAN)

You have way too many people in your van. Why are you in this area anyway?

DAN

Sir we are just out enjoying the summer night and checking out the night life.

POLICE OFFICER (TO DAN)

Get back in your ride and sit tight!
[Dan proceeds to get back in the van and wait. All his friends are joking and saying he is going away, he is up the creek. He is getting a ticket.]

DAN

Okay guys keep it down he is coming back. Keep it down so I can hear what he says.

POLICE OFFICER (TO DAN)

Okay I am citing you for excessive number of occupants in the vehicle. I want you to turn this truck around and go back to Mission Hill or where ever you came from and unload your guest. You need to pay this fine or show up in court. If you fail to show we will come and get you. Understood!

DAN

Yes sir, sir!

POLICE OFFICER (TO DAN)

ARE YOU MAKING FUN OF ME???

DAN (HOLDING BACK HIS LAUGH) No sir! Sir!

POLICE OFFICER (TO DAN) OK SCRAM! REMEMBER WHAT I SAID!!!!

BABE (TO DAN)

Okay Dan let us know when take him to court. We will be YOUR witnesses. Bye the way did Barry tell you all of us are going to the Marine Recruiter in the morning? Do you want to come?

DAN

You guys going to enlist in the Marine Corps. Cool! Okay I will go with you and also let you know when the court date comes up. (Stephanie over hears the Marine Corps conversation)

[Dan has a brainstorm. He hates traditional school since his deafness and elementary school year experiences -- He has decided to get real time law experience to find out if he wants to be a lawyer. He reads, reads, and reads at the Boston Public Library on how to win court cases. He test his ability to defend himself by speeding and getting tickets and so on. All in the name of Attorney self-development. Dan prints up the date/time/court he has to attend and hands out invite flyers to all his friends at the Boston Public Library, Kids in Roslindale, Mission Hill, Hyde Park and West Roxbury and a few ex-girlfriends.]
[They think oh he is going to be a star!! Someone they can call on.]

EXT. DEDHAM MALL PARKING LOT - VANISHING POINT VAN – 7:00PM [SUMMER EVENING]

[Dan peels out of the parking lot onto the highway. Music is cranked. Dedham police peel out of the fast food parking lot just after the van passes them. They chase the van to border of Boston. The unique painting the van is very is to identify. Although the van crosses the border the Dedham police alert the Boston police.]

[Within minutes a Transit Authority [female] police officer pulls up behind the van and flips on the blue lights and siren. Dan slows down to a stop. A very pretty TA police lady walks up and ask for license and registration. Never seeing a TA police car before Dan begins to debate her.]

DAN

Aren't you out of your juristdiction?

[The TA Police officer stops and stares a Dan. Mimics with her mouth and index finger to say "one minute" Shaking her head]

(all of a sudden 10 State Police cars come barreling down the highway surrounding Dan.

DAN

Oh shit…….(Fades from scene)

[ONE YEAR LATER] Stephanie and Dan have been dating for one year. Still getting to know each other and getting on each other's nerves etc.]

Stephanie the Greek girlfriend from hell!

CHAPTER FIVE

PLAN B – LEGAL TRAINING KIND OF…

EXT. Evening - Dan and Stephanie are in Dan's van when Dan suddenly notice a little old lady getting robbed 6:30pm on Longwood Avenue Boston.

DAN

Did you see that?

STEPHANIE

See what? No I missed it

DAN

(Pointing at the windshield)Over there that guy, those kids in that car just knocked over that little old lady and stole her pocket book.

STEPHANIE

Just let it go!

(As Dan skids up to the action the gang kids jump into a small Toyota and left the old lady laying on the street. Dan jumps out to help the old lady up and says he will be right back - the chase begins)

STEPHANIE

Just let it go! What are you gonna do there are 4 of them?

DAN

Hang on! Put your seatbelt on!

(Dan is searching for a weapon or anything he can use to get the pocket book back. As the chase is going and the van is swerving up and down on the side streets - Dan find a 15 inch pipe baton under the drivers seat and pulls it out fast hitting Stephanie on the head.)

(Bam!!)

STEPHANIE

Aarrrrrgh you just hit me in the head!!!

DAN

Here hold this for me.

(Handing her the baton)

(Dan finally rams the Toyota and the gang throws the pocketbook out the window) Dan skids to a halt jumps out to retrieve the pocket book. Stephanie is holding her head. Dan pulls over to a pizza place that has closed for the night. There are two Boston cops inside eating. Dan bangs on the locked door. The owner scrambles with many keys to open the door.)

(The door opens)

DAN

Officers I just chased a gang that robbed a little old lady on Longwood Ave like 10 minutes ago. This is her pocket book with all her stuff - If you could please return it to her.(Handing the bag over)

BP OFFICER

Ok thanks but what happened to her (pointing at Stephanie holding her swollen head.)

DAN

Oh she's okay just something in her eye.

(Stephanie hands the license plate number to the BPO)

[Dan is letting Stephanie stay over his apartment where he lives with his dad. Even his dad thinks she is a gorgeous fruit cake - nutty and all that. Few marbles missing - lights are on but nobody is home.]

EXT. 103 CALUMENT STREET MISSION HILL HOUSE--EVENING

[Standing on Dan's front porch talking]

DAN (TO STEPHANIE)

Stephanie I know you want to stay over tonight but I really have to get up early for court. Besides I want to tell you need to be a little bit quieter in the house. Both my dad and landlord have said you make too much noise. You close the cabinet doors to loud, you don't pick up your feet when you walk. It is just a bit much...... so you have to go home.

STEPHANIE

Awww Dan you know I love you. Please let me stay. I promise I will be really. I can understand becoming a Lawyer thing but the Marines? Why do you want to be a Marine?

DAN (TO STEPHANIE)

I don't mind to take an oath to support and defend the Constitution of the United States. I would do so honorably to serve this great nation. It is not like I have felt the burning sting of bullet and shrapnel or that I have heard the unforgettable and frightening sounds of incoming shells but I feel like in a past life I served before. I feel like I at one time had rows of ribbons on my chest served courageously. I can't quite explain it my willingness—my patriotic willingness to risk my life imbued with the passion of patriotism. I don't fantasize about being the President, vice President, a member of Congress. Maybe the head the National Security Council or CIA - that is what I would work towards after a 30 year career in the Marines. I can't explain it but it

is just in my blood.
I care deeply about people and believe that the interests of our country would be better if I advance to a high level marine. Please recognize that our nation is at risk in a dangerous world. I must act accordingly and in my opinion succeeded, in advancing the cause of world peace by strengthening our country, an Army of one among a band of brothers acting to restore and sustain democracy throughout the world, and by having the courage to take decisive action when needed.

Do you watch the news at all? Do you ever watch War Stories?

STEPHANIE
Yes, I know we won at Pearl Harbor

DAN
Aye yi! yi! Not exactly. So please you have to go home tonight.

Ya know almost every war or military action with the exception of world war 2 I believe is inevitable that the Congress will, in the end, blame the Executive Branch. But I suggest to you that it is the Congress which must accept at least some of the blame in the case of freedom-fighters.

Plain and simple, the Congress is to blame because of the fickle, vacillating, unpredictable, on-again-off-again policy toward democratic resistance, the so-called "commandos of freedom."

Do you ever read books?

STEPHANIE
Ya sometimes

DAN
I do not believe that the support of worldwide freedom fighters can be treated as the passage of a budget. I suppose if the budget doesn't get passed on time again this year, there will be inevitably another extension of a month or two. But the freedom fighters, are people -- living, breathing, young men and women -- who have had to suffer a desperate struggle for liberty, with sporadic and confusing support from the

United States of America. Armies need food and consistent help. They need a flow of money, of arms, clothing, and medical supplies.

And that's what I am about -a strong defense to shine a light on freedom, stability, and the law of war!!!

STEPHANIE

What the hell are you talking about? Do you want something to eat?

DAN

The Congress of the United States allowed the President to encourage them to do battle and then abandoned them. The Congress of the United States left soldiers in the field unsupported and vulnerable to their Communist enemies for example in Vietnam. It does not make sense to me.
So please Stephanie you have to go home tonight. I need to read more and then get some sleep.

DAN

Stephanie even your voice is naturally loud. Please, please, please. (Stephanie pushing back with her hands)

DAN

No! No! Not tonight……I need to get this law experience in case I cannot get into the Marine Corps. I need the law training to be a lawyer - something to fall back on.

[Dan picks up Stephanie over his shoulder and carries her down the front steps - opens her passenger car door. Puts her in, turns and races up the six steps on the front porch, opens the front exterior door, races down the hallway to the apartment door. Gets inside and slams it shut. He looks up at the top of the door and notices it didn't shut. He opens a bit and slams again. Same-thing. He looks down and there is Stephanie on her hands and knees (she had crawled in behind Dan) and put her hand in the door to stop Dan from shutting and locking it.]

STEPHANIE

AAAAAAAAAARRRRRRRRGGGGGGGGGGGG!! YOU BROKE MY FINGERS!!!! OWWOWOWOWOWOWOWOWOWO OOOOOHHHH.

DAN (TO STEPHANIE)

What did you doooo? Why did you do that??? What kind of idiot sticks her hand in the door to stop it from shutting? How am I supposed to know you did that?

STEPHANIE
Oohhhh look you broke my fingers.

DAN
No I didn't it'll be just fine. Go ahead sleep on the sofa.

STEPHANIE
But my fingers? Look you broke my fingers. Do you think they are broken?

DAN
Naw they'er ok just a little bent. They will be fine in the morning. So go ahead go to sleep.
[Dan's Dad peeks down the hallway and mimmicks laughing.

[Dan walks to the kitchen where he and his dad are chuckling to themselves. LOL]

DAN (TO HIS DAD)
Geeezzz!! Did you see what she did? Is she crazy? She put her fricking fingers in the door to stop the door - who does that!!!

[Early next morning]

DAN (CALLING OUT)
Stephanie, Stephanie - dad where is she?

DAN'S DAD
Stephanie work up early and drove herself to the hospital. Oh and by the way she told me to tell you to leave the toilet seat down.

DAN
Okay great she is out. I have to get to court to fight this ticket. Stephanie said to leave the toilet seat down? Is she crazy?

DAN'S DAD
She is crazy I wish you would dump her. She doesn't want to sleep alone at her place that is why she keeps coming over here. Please, please find someone else.

DAN
Okay I'll work on it but she is not that bad......   gotta go!

[Visual - Dan is handing out Xeroxed page to invite all his friends and family to watch him dispute his moving violation tickets (it is also a fundraising tactic as everyone is betting on who wins the case - Dan or Police Officers)].

FRANK (THE PERKULATOR)

Okay place your bets here - whose gonna win Dan or the Commonwealth of Massachusetts?

[Kids betting cash with Frank P.]

Moving Vehicle Case 1 montage

Moving Vehicle Case 2 montage

Moving Vehicle Case 3 montage

[Dan shows up late for court. He arrives 3 minutes late and the court guard will not let him in. He also has to go to the bathroom. Quickly runs around the corner to the men's room. Opens the door heads to the handicap stall. He has a hand full of documents and a briefcase. He sits down and tries to collect his thoughts to represent himself. Handicap man in an electric wheelchair rolls in. He yells into the stall where Dan is sitting.]

WHEELCHAIR GUY (PLAYED BY A JACK BLACK TYPE)

Hey you in there! Do you have some kind of disability? Have a cane or wheelchair?

DAN

Yes sir I do but I will be right out!!

WHEELCHAIR GUY
(YELLING)

COME ON GET OUT OF THERE RIGHT NOW!! I AM A GREEN BERET!! DAMMIT I

SERVED NAM!! I am the only one in this courthouse with a disability! No respect! No respect I swear!
[Wheel chair guy takes cane and puts it under the stall door. He hooks Dan's right ankle and begin to roll backwards with his electric wheelchair. Then sideways dragging Dan from side to side using the wheelchair.]

DAN
OH YEAH AND I AM DEAF BASTARD!!! NOW GET THIS CANE THE HELL OF MY FOOT!!HEY WHOA!!! WHAT THE HELL!!!! KNOOCK IT OFF!!! GET OFF ME!!! !!
[Dan holds up his hearing above the stall door]

WHEELCHAIR GUY
A HEARING AID!!!! That's no disability! GET THE HELL OUT OF THERE OR I AM GOING SHIT THRU THE CRACK OF THIS DOOR. COME ON GET THE HELL OUT OF THERE

DAN
[YELLING FROM THE OTHERSIDE OF STALL DOOR] WHADDA YA MEAN NOT A DISABILITY? THEY WON'T LET ME SERVE! I CAN'T JOIN THE POLICE FORCE! I CAN'T GET ANY JOB THAT I WANT!!!!!!!!!!!!!!!

[Dan opens the stall door AND HOLDS IT OPEN WHILE saluting the green beret wheel chair guy]

DAN
Regardless of your issues - Sir I salute you and want to thank you for your service to our country

WHEELCHAIR GUY
(RUSHES INTO THE STALL)

DEAF BASTARD JUST Get out of my way! NO I DON'T HAVE ISSUE I JUST HAVE TO TAKE A (BLEEP)

DAN
(PONDERING TURNS HEAD TO THE LEFT - HOW DID HE KNOW I AM DEAF BASTARD?)

[Dan showed up late for court. Still trying to figure out how to get into the court room. He puts his right hand on the wall and with his other hand he scratches his ankle. His right hand accidentally hits the fire alarm. WHOOP WHOOOP WHOOOP!!! The overhead speaker "please head to the nearest exit".]
[Ten minutes later the all clear is sounded and Dan slips into the courtroom with all the other people. The case that was in motion before the alarm is proceeding….]

JUDGE
(TO THE DEFENDANT)
Now please explain to the court why you hit Mr. Dempsy with a hammer?

DEFENDANT (WISEGUY)
Your honor I was being nice - it was a rubber hammer!
[Camera flashes to beat-up guy all black and blue in bandages.]

DEFENDANT (WISEGUY)
Your honor among other things like the money he owes me. I asked him -- what kinda work he does? He told me he is a meteorologist. An FN meteorologist! I said if you can tell me the correct weather and I bet my team on it to win -- your honor forgatta bouttt it --this guy is an idiot

He guessed wrong. Yes your honor a rubber hammer - I didn't want to hurt him LOL
[Court room laughs]

JUDGE (TO COURTROOM)
Ok we will continue this case to the 19th of the month. Next up Commonwealth vs Daniel Shea. Mr. Shea please raise your right hand. Do you swear to tell the truth the whole truth and nothing but the truth?

DAN
I do.

[As Dan is standing up in front of the court the two doors swing open. Rolling in dripping wet [from the toilet overflowing] is the guy in the electric wheel chair. He rolls all the way to the front of the court room and parks on the left. He apparently is the District Attorney (court prosecutor). Dan will have to debate him from time to time.]
[Dan thinking to himself - Yikes! What a really bad first impression. Fighting with a wheelchair guy who is the prosecutor -Dan realizes.]
[The camera flashes to several scenes where Dan is in the court representing himself. Judge repeats *"Case Dismissed!"* Prosecutor and police both develop respect for Dan's amateur self- representation. After all it is only moving violations speeding etc. In the 1980s radar and speed traps were really not present.]

[Photo collage of tickets, Dan's speaking in court, Judge's dismisses by banging the gavel.] ***(FLASH - DISMISSED! (x3)***

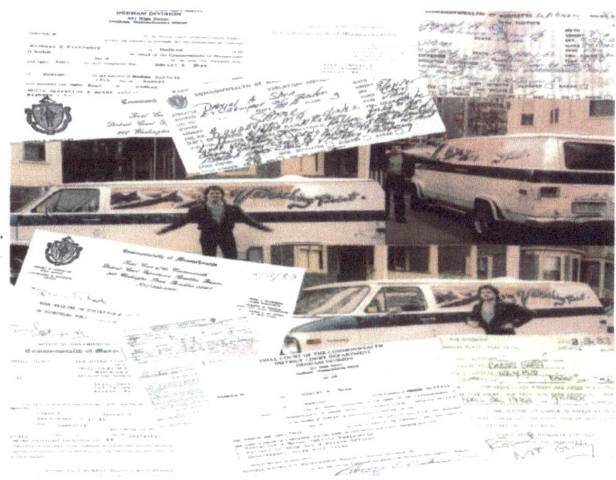

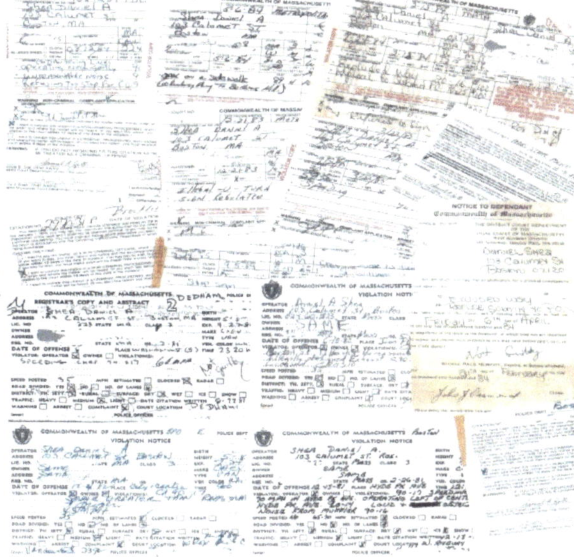

[ALL RISE]

FEMALE JUDGE (TO DAN)

Mr. Shea it appears you have quite a large following here in court today.

DAN (TO COURTROOM)

You are absolutely correct your honor. In this side of the room I have my cousins from Mission Hill, friends from Roslindale, Hyde Park, West Roxbury and Dedham. On this side of the room - my friends from the hood (ahem) excuse me Roxbury, my amigos from Jamaica Plain and that little old lady of there is my grandmother.

FEMALE JUDGE (TO DAN)

It would be in your best interest that they keep quiet! No talking! No whooting! No high fiving! First sign of disobedience in my court you will go straight to the slammer for contempt. Do

I make myself clear? There is also a rumor going around that some form of gambling is taking place in regards to your hearings - be warned there will be no gambling in this courtroom!

DAN (TO COURTROOM)
Geesh your honor lighten up this is just a moving violation.

FEMALE JUDGE (TO DAN)
Mr. Shea you've been warned.

DAN (TO JUDGE)
Your honor if I passed intersection 1, intersection 2, and intersection 3. and based on the distance, rate of speed one at lease one of those lights would have been red by the time I went trhu the intersection. Yet the officer only cited me for speeding 40 miles an hour in a 30 mile an hour speed zone. Yet I was never cited for running a red light. Now common sense would tell you that speed was not really high passing through this range of space so based on the common sense evidence - either the officer was colored blind or I was really going slower than he estimated mind you he was not using radar. I rest my case.

FEMALE JUDGE (TO DAN)
[CASE NUMBER XXXX TBD FILL IN
Based on the common sense evidence - case dismissed.

[Dan's friends are all clapping]

DAN (TO COURTROOM)
.--- That's the way I roll!!! [Dan adjust his tie] CAN I GET A WHAT!WHAT! BEAT -- MUSIC FADES IN)

"Can I Get A..."

[Jay-Z]

Bounce wit me, wit me, wit me wit me
Can you bounce wit me, bounce wit me, wit me wit me
Can you bounce wit me, bounce wit me, ge-gi-gi-gi-gi-gi
Can you bounce wit me, bounce wit me, ye-ye-yeah
Uh-huh uh-huh bounce wit me, bounce wit me
Can ya can ya can ya bounce wit me, bounce wit me
Ya-yah-yah, ya-ya-yah-yeah bounce wit me, bounce wit me
Ge-gi, ge-gi-gi-gi-geyeah bounce wit me,

bounce wit me
Get it!
[Verse One: Jay-Z]
Can I hit in the MORNIN
without givin you half of my dough
And even worse if I was broke would you WANT ME?
If I couldn't get you finer things
like all of them diamond rings bitches KILL FOR
would you STILL ROLL?
If we couldn't see the sun risin off the shore of Thailand
would you RIDE THEN, if I wasn't DRIVIN?

[BABE FARTS AND EVERYONE RUNS OUT OF THE COURT ROOM]

CHAPTER SIX

GETTING RECRUITED

(INT. FLASH BOSTON PUBLIC LIBRARY - BOOK CASES AND TABLE)
[Camera pans back and forth as Dan continues flipping thru books to enhance his knowledge]

(EXT. DAN WALKING FROM LIBRARY TO HIS VAN. GETS IN AND DRIVES TO ROSLINDALE)

(Dan drives around looking for his friend Babe. Dan slowly drive up to a single family home that Babe is cutting the grass. Babe has head phones on as he is cutting.)

DAN (TO BABE)
Babe!

(Babe turns off the lawn mower)

BABE
Hey whatz up?

DAN (TO BABE)
I thought you guys said you were going to the recruiting office today?

BABE
Oh yeah as soon as I am done here we are.

(Kitty - owner of the house Babe is working on is an Oversized African American female who has a crush on Babe. Babe is only working for the money)

KITTY
Babe honey can you do me a favor?

KITTY
Babe honey can you do me a favor?

KITTY
I just need you to trim my bush.

(Dan and Babe are stunned)

BABE
What bush?

KITTY
The one right here behind the front door. I am afraid someone will hide there and attack me.

BABE
Don't worry about it. No one is going to bother your fat asssss.

KITTY
No really I am afraid.

BABE
Don't worry about it. Just carry an AXE. No one will mess with you. Come on Dan we gotta go.

(Dan & Babe get in the van and drive away)

INT. USMC RECRUITING STATION - DAY

[Dan and his friends show up at the Norwood Mass USMC Recruiting Station. The recruiters are elated that so many of Dan's friends showed up.]

USMC RECRUITER 1 (TO GROUP)
Okay guys settle down, settle down. I need you all to fill this paperwork so grab a clip board and answer all the questions. Just to let you know after we do the paperwork tomorrow YOU NEED TO SHOW UP AT THE Barns Building Military Entrance Processing Station, known at 495 Summer Street 4th Floor stop by the MP's desk and sign in so they know your there. There is NO PARKING so best if you take the train to South Station.

Here is what you can expect during your processing. At the processing center you will be tested for drugs, you must undergo Physical examinations that are vitally important because everyone entering the armed forces must be in good health to endure the challenges of basic training and military service. You will have to remove your outer clothing during parts of the examination. Your physical examination consists of:

- Height and weight measurements
- Hearing and vision examinations
- Urine and blood tests
- Drug and alcohol tests
- Muscle group and joint maneuvers, in underclothing
- Complete physical examination and interview
- Specialized test if required

Each applicant for military service is required to take the CAT-ASVAB, which measures aptitude in a broad range of career fields. Does anyone here were glasses? Have hearing issues?

[Dan raises his hand in front of all his friends and a few other guys signing up.]

USMC RECRUITER 1 (TO DAN & GROUP)

Okay you with your hand raised come over to my office. The rest of you keep on working on the paperwork.

USMC RECRUITER 1 (TO DAN)

What is the issue hearing or eyes?

DAN

Well it is my hearing. I am wearing a hearing aid.

USMC RECRUITER 1 (TO DAN)

And how bad is it? How bad is your loss? We have guys all the time with glasses and hearing aids. Okay what here a moment. First Sergeant please come here a moment I have a question to ask you.

FIRST SERGEANT (TO USMC RECRUITER 1)

Yes what can I do for you?

USMC RECRUITER 1 (TO FIRST SERGEANT)

I would like you to meet Daniel Shea he is interested in signing up with all his friends out there in our classroom. Dan has a hearing issue that might be a problem when he gets to MEPS. Dan tell us why you would make a good Marine?

DAN (TO FIRST SERGEANT)
Yes well my Dad was a marine, my uncle served. I am in good health and I want……

[Interrupted by loud obnoxious Jock Marine walking in the room]

USMC JOCK RECRUITER (LOUD OBNOXIOUS)
Gents how are we doing today!! Man I feel good. Had a great work out.

FIRST SERGEANT (TO DAN)
Okay here is what I want you to do. When you get to the MEPS I want you to take off your hearing aid and put it in your pocket. Just try to get through in-processing that way.

DAN (TO FIRST SERGEANT)
Just put it in my pocket. Okay, I can do that.

[FADE TO BLACK]

(INT. SOUTH STATION METRO ESCALATORS—EARLY MORNING)
>FLASH GROUP 1 REGULAR CUTIES
>FLASH GROUP 2 CHEERLEADERS
>FLASH GROUP 3 SWEDE TOURIST GIRLS

[It is the day after leaving the recruiting station. The group is supposed to show up at the MEPS Marine Entrance Processing station on Summer Street downtown Boston. Riding on the "upward" bound escalators they keep getting side tracked by inbound beauties riding on the "down escalators" the escalators. They each hold up their finger to rate the girls 1 thru 10. 10 being the hotest. The first group are ordinary girls that invite the guys to brunch. Second group are cheerleaders - the guys just get off the up escalator and start going down after rating the girls. Third attempt - they meet (to good to be true) a Swedish tourist group. Eventually they make to the MEPS building - 3 days later.]

[Song kicks on during the escalator ride - GORILLAS BY FEEL GOOD INC.]

Chorus Repeats…….

Haha haha haha haha
Haha haha haha haha ha

Feel good
Feel good
Feel good
Feel good
Feel good

City's breakin' down on a camel's back
They just have to go 'cos they don't know when
So all you fill the streets it's appealing to see
You won't get out the county, 'cos you're bad and free

Shit, I'm stepping in the heart of this here
(Here)
Care bear reppin' in the heart of this here
(Here)
Watch me as I gravitate
Haha haha ha

Yo, we goin' to ghost town, this Motown
With yo' sound you in the blink
Gon' bite the dust, can't fight with us
With your sound you kill the Inc.

So, don't stop, get it, get it
(Get it)
Until you're cheddar header
Watch the way I navigate
Haha haha ha

Feel good
Feel good
Feel good

Feel good

Haha haha ha

INT. RIDING THE METRO TRAIN 3RD TRIP TO MEPS BUILDING

(Third trip to downtown Boston - just before they exit the train and meet the Swedish tourist group Joey Ballentine is standing up in the train. Passengers are in a tight standing room. Joey begins small talk with the 18 year old gum chewing girl with a bad acne problem standing next to him.)

JOEY BALLENTINE (TO 18 YEO GIRL)
Hey, Hey how you doing? Nice tits..

18 YEO GIRL(ROLLS HER EYES)

[DAN WHISPERS INTO JOEY'S EAR]

JOEY BALLENTINE (TO 18 YEO GIRL)
Hey nice green neon shirt [kinder more subtle approach].

[Guys are snickering and so are other passengers.]

18 YEO GIRL
[smiles while flaunting her cleevage]

JOEY BALENTINE (TO 18 YEO GIRL)
Here, here is my number call me later and I'll help you out. Guys this is our stop. See you in 4 years when I get out of the Marines. Gotta gooooo!!

[GROUP RUNNING TO BARNES BUILDING]
(EXT/INT. ENTRANCE MEPS BUILDING – EARLY MORNING)

MILITARY POLICE (MP)
Name?

BABE (TO MP)
Sir, my name is William Appleday but my friends call me "Babe?

MILITARY POLICE (MP)
Oh they do - do they BABE!

BABE (TO MP)
Babe, you know like Babe Ruth

MILITARY POLICE (MP)
Are you with these other guys? Did you sign up as group?

BABE (TO MP)
Yeah we did there is X of us.

MILITARY POLICE (MP) [Looking at his clip board]You guys were supposed to be here three days ago!

BABE (TO MP)
Yeah well there were these cheerleaders, and then there was a going away party, and then there was…….

MILITARY POLICE (MP) [interrupting]
SHUT UP!! Listen this ain't the boy scouts you guys were expected three days ago. You guys are celebrating and you're not even in the service yet!! Go stand over there!

[This is their first 1st try as a group to get into the Marine Corps. Dan is in line in a row with 50 other guys waiting to be called. As he gets closer to the nurse sitting at the desk the guy in front of him steps to the side after answering all her questions. Dan quickly slips his hearing aid off his ear and into his pocket. He steps forward. Thinking he would read the nurse's lips - her head is facing the desk (looking down) and he doesn't realize she is reading the questions. He has no idea she is talking.]

MILITARY POLICE (MP)
[sneaks up and slaps Dan on the back]

WAKE UP! WAKE UP! Answer her questions. We haven't got all day.

[everyone is starring]

MEPS NURSE
What's the matter can't you hear me?

DAN (TO NURSE)
Okay wait a minute I have to put this on.

[reaches into his pocket and puts the hearing aid on]

MEPS NURSE
Are you deaf?

DAN (TO NURSE)
Half deaf.

MEPS NURSE
Okay go stand in that line and we'll get you tested.

[Dan is asked to step into a sound proof booth with ten other guys. He puts the head phones on and picks up a device that has a red button. Each time he hears a sounds he is to push the button. He figures he will watch the guy next to him and push when the other guy pushes his button.
Test begins. Pushing away on the button - the Marine looking thru the window on the sound proof door yells thru Dan's head phones - KEEP YOUR HEAD STRAIGHT!!!!]
As Dan exits the processing area another Marine recruiter approaches him.

MARINE (HALLWAY)
Hey man you look all disappointed and

whatnot. Whats the deal?

DAN (TO HALLWAY MARINE)
I didn't pass the hearing test.
MARINE (HALLWAY)
Look man don't give up! The nurses change shift and so does everyone else. You just have to keep trying and hang in there. Lots of guys get in with issues. There are 500 guys a day coming thru here. They are not going to remember you. Do you drive?

DAN (TO HALLWAY MARINE)
No not right now.

MARINE (HALLWAY)
Give me your address and me and my buddy will pick you up in the morning. We have a couple of new recruits we have to pick up as well. Different day - another chance. Whadday say?

DAN (TO HALLWAY MARINE)
Okay here is my address - what time?

MARINE (HALLWAY)
5:00am - and look maybe I can get my friend she is a nurse to sit in at the front desk. Possibly no hearing test at all.

DAN (TO HALLWAY MARINE)
That would be frikkin grreatttttt!!!!! 5:00am don't forget me!!

Dan and the Marine high-five…..

<u>(EXT. ENTRANCE MEPS BUILDING – LATE AFTERNOON)</u>
[Dan and friend meet up with his friends outside the MEPS building.]

DAN (TO GROUP)
Hey guys how's it going?

NICKY (TO GROUP)
We all got in - did you?

DAN (TO GROUP)
Naw not yet. I am going to have to come back again. They told me I have to wait at least 24hrs.

NICKY (TO GROUP)
Well don't worry man we are all going to stick with you until you get in. Right guys?

GROUP (TOGETHER)
Yes were with you man!!

(EXT. FRONT DOOR - DAN'S HOUSE – 5:00AM)

[As promised the next morning the Marines show up at Dan's house at 5:00am. They ring the bell several times. Stephanie has no idea who is ringing the bell. Dan can't hear the doorbell without his hearing aid. Stephanie is not a morning person and is pissed from the annoying doorbell.]

STEPHANIE (TO THE MARINES)
WHAT!! WHO ARE YOU?

MARINE 1
Sorry madam for waking you up. Dan Shea had asked us to pick him up on the way to the processing station this morning. Is he awake?

STEPHANIE
Oh oh that's right I'm sorry. He changed his mind he said he is not going.

MARINE 1
Excuse me? Not going?
[Marines look at each other]

STEPHANIE
Yes that's right not going. He doesn't want to go.

MARINE 2
Ok madam. Again pardon us for ringing the bell so early.

[Stephanie closes the door ever so quietly and sneaks back into bed with Dan]

(INT. BEDROOM - DAN'S HOUSE LATER THAT MORNING– 9:00AM)

DAN
[kicking of the blankets]
What! What! what time is it? Stephanie what time is it?

STEPHANIE
Its too early that's what time it is. Go back to sleep

DAN
[Launching out of the bed to find a clock]No really I have to get up I have an appointment today. Did anyone ring the bell?

STEPHANIE
No. Come on get back in the bed.

DAN
No this is something got to do. I need a life I can't hang around here forever I gotta get down to the Marine recruiting station. I'll catch you later.

ADD IN STEPHANI TAKES MARINES NEXT DOOR TO 2 18 YEAROLDS THEY HAND FEED THE MARINES… I THINK SHE LOVES ME. THE GIRLS TRYING TO STALL THE GUYS….. OH I LOVE A GUY IN UNIFORM. WE ARE CHEERLEADERS AND WE ARE GOINGTO DO A CHEER

GIVE ME AN M AN I RIANES.

GUYS ARE LOOKING AT THE WATCH - WE GOTTAGOKKKKKKKKKKKKKKKKKKKKKKKKKKKKKKKKKKK KKKKKKKKK

EXT/INT. ENTRANCE MEPS BUILDING – NOON

MILITARY POLICE (MP)
Name?

DAN
Dan Shea

MILITARY POLICE (MP)
You are not on the list. Who is your recruiter? We are pretty much done for the day. If you were to in-process you need to be here 5:00am or just shortly thereafter.

DAN
Okay I'll come back.

MILITARY POLICE (MP)
Okay no wait I see your name here from a day ago. Ok I know who your recruiter is. Want me to have him pick you up in the morning?

DAN
Okay yes that would be great.

MILITARY POLICE (MP)
Okay I'll reach out to him by phone. Be ready bright and early.

DAN
Yes sir, will do.

(EXT. FRONT DOOR - DAN'S HOUSE – 5:00AM)

(As promised the next morning the same Marines show up at Dan's house at 5:00am AGAIN. They ring the bell several times. Again Dan can't hear the doorbell without his hearing aid. Stephanie wakes up. Slides out of bed quietly and answers the door while Dan is sound asleep.)

STEPHANIE (TO THE MARINES)
Hello! Hello! Please stop ringing the bell!

MARINES
Sorry madam for waking you up. Dan Shea had asked us to pick him up on the way to the processing station this morning. Is he awake?

STEPHANIE
No he never came home last night. He must have stayed over his friend's house. Why are you here?

MARINE 1
Dan had requested a ride to the MEPS building for in-processing to the Corps.

STEPHANIE (TO THE MARINES)
Oh noooo. He changed his mind. You know he always does that I Just can't keep focused you know. Anyway no need to hang around he is just not marine material. You yell duck!! And he'll say "What?"

MARINES[Marines look at each other-in disbelief]

STEPHANIE (TO THE MARINES)
Yes that's right not going…..goodbye!

MARINES
Ok madam. Again pardon us for ringing the bell so early.

[Stephanie closes the door ever so quietly and sneaks back into bed with Dan]

(INT. BEDROOM – DAN'S HOUSE – 8:00AM)

DAN
[kicking of the blankets] [opening the shades/curtains]
NOOOOOOoooo What! What! what time is it? Stephanie what time is it?

STEPHANIE
TURN OFF THE LIGHTS!! TURN OFF THE LIGHTS!!!

DAN
What lights? That's the sun…

STEPHANIE
Go back to sleep!

DAN[Leaping out of the bed to find a clock] No really I have to get up I have an appointment today. Did anyone ring the bell?

STEPHANIE
NO!!!! No one showed up!!!!

DAN
[running around to get dressed -talking to aloud to himself]

Okay its 8:00am I can still make it. I can still make it.

[Dan is picking up the phone and dialing]

DAN [ON THE PHONE]
DID YOU GET IT? DID YOU GET IT? DID YOU GET MY CHECK YET?

[Dan SLAMS DOWN THE PHONE and picks the phone up again and dialing]

DAN [ON THE PHONE]
DID YOU GET IT? DID YOU GET IT? DID YOU GET MY CHECK YET?

STEPHANIE
Who are you calling so early in the morning?

DAN
My bill collectors -- I call them everyday to wake them up and ask if they got my check yet.

STEPHANIE
Did you send them a check?

DAN
No but I want them to keep checking the mail….its an ongoing relationship

(EXT. SOUTH STATION - SUMMER STREET – 10:00AM)
[Running up the escalator - ignoring all the well endowed girls going down the "down" escalator. Dan bolts out of the train station running down the sidewalk. Jumps over a dog walking by. Jumps over a volts wagon beetle. Runs into the Barnes building MEPS front door.]

MILITARY POLICE (MP)
Name?

DAN
Dan Shea

MILITARY POLICE (MP)

Oh yea from the other day. Let me guess you missed your ride.

DAN

No sir they never showed.

MILITARY POLICE (MP)

No I don't think so. If a Marine say he going to be there. Then he is going to be there.

DAN

My girlfriend said no one rang the doorbell.

MILITARY POLICE (MP)

Your girlfriend-- Man that is the oldest trick in the book. You know your girlfriend don't want you to leave. Hold up. I will get your recruiter he is still around in the building somewhere. You can ask him yourself.

[begins to call the recruiter on the phone]

DAN

Ok

[Recruiter - the Hall Marine shows up in the lobby with a visitors ID in his hand]

HALLWAY MARINE

Mr. Shea good to see you. Welcome back.

DAN

Glad to be back. Just one quick question - did you meet Stephanie?

HALLWAY MARINE

Is Stephanie the one who answers your door at 5:00am? Then yes! Put this ID on and walk with me.

DAN

Dammit! She said no one rang the bell!!!

HALLWAY MARINE

Go ahead and get in the line and we see you on the other side of the wall.

[Standing in line with several other guys in front and behind Dan. There is an athletic type jock in line. Making loud jokes. Every so many minutes you hear a group in the line laughing in monotone. Dan could quite hear the deaf jokes.)

CHAPTER SEVEN

I'M BAD!

(**EXT. DAYTIME - DOWNTOWN BOSTON - BANK ENTRANCE)**

(Dan and Babe just depart the USMC Barnes building. Walking and talking Dan is enraged and explaining to Babe about how Stephanie interfered with the USMC Recruiters.]

DAN
Babe Dammit! Can you believe she would do such a thing!!!

BABE
I know I believe it. I told you she wasn't good for you.

DAN
I am so pissed I just want to scream! It is hard enough that I have to wear this thing on my ear everyday, that I can't get on the police force, I can't do what I what to do for work and then she goes and almost screws up my future with the Marine Corps.

BABE
All I know is I told you. Hey come with me to the bank for a minute I just have to cash this check and then we'll go eat.

DAN
Okay okay - just hold me back if look like I am going to punch somebody's lights out.

[Walking up the steps and into the Bank's revolving door]

BABE [TO DAN]
[Outside bank revolving door] Hey wait watch this…..

[Babe walks into the revolving door and comes back outside 1, 2, 3 times]

DAN[TO BABE]
What are you doing?

[People exiting the bank revolving door with a nasty look on their face]

BABE [TO DAN]
I am timing my farts with the revolving door. No need to waste a perfectly good fart.

[Babe laughs like Bevis and Butthead]

DAN[TO BABE]

Yea but now I have to go with you in the bank.

[Dan takes a seat near an old guy. Babe walks up to the teller. Standing in line are two odd looking gentleman with large gym bags (one white guy and one African male). All of a sudden out comes the guns]

WHITE BANK ROBBER

Okay okay - EVERYONE JUST SIT TIGHT WHILE WE DO A LITTLE WITHDRAWL OVER HERE.

BLACK BANK ROBBER

Okay okay - YOU HEARD WHAT THE MAN SAID - SIT TIGHT! GET DOWN! GET DOWN! WHAT ARE YOU LOOKING AT! YOU DON'T KNOW ME - GET DOWN DOWN THATS RIGHT!!

[Already fuming from Stephanie and now this. Dan is shaking his head in disbelief. He reacts quickly. Dan grabs a few items (his cane, hat and cigar) from the old guy that was sitting next to him (now on the floor). From the ash tray Dan powders his mustace with white ash to look like an old guy. Bent over he is walking in character as an old guy with a hat, cane, cigar - and he heads up to the teller as if he is unaware that a robbery is in progress.]

BLACK BANK ROBBER

Hello! Hello EXCUSE ME!! Sir do you hear me?

[Dan is mumbling gibberish. Babe is shaking his head in disbelief. Dan ignores the bank robber and all the people on the floor are watching.]

WHITE BANK ROBBER

Hey old man!! Hello! Hello EXCUSE ME SIR - (Humoring Dan)
How can I help you today?

DAN AS OLD MAN

(Mumbles softy) wait for it…. (all the bank is asking "what did he say?")

WHITE BANK ROBBER

What? I CAN'T HEAR YOUUUU!!!!

DAN AS OLD MAN

(Repeats softy) wait for it…. (and rips a fart really loud) [Whole bank together - EEEWWWWW!!]

[ACTION: Just then --like lightening Dan cracks the cane across the White Bank Robbers face and knocks him out and grabs his gun. Just as the Black Bank robber had walked over - Dan points the gun in his face and takes away his gun.

DAN AS OLD MAN (Dan yells at the Black Bank Robber and orders him to moon walk)

DO THE MOON WALK!

(Micheal Jackson's song fades in - *I'm Bad I'm Bad)*

"Bad"
Because I'm Bad, I'm Bad-
Come On
(Bad Bad-Really, Really Bad)
You Know I'm Bad, I'm Bad-
You Know It
(Bad Bad-Really, Really Bad)
You Know I'm Bad, I'm Bad-
Come On, You Know
(Bad Bad-Really, Really Bad)
And The Whole World Has To
Answer Right Now
Just To Tell You Once Again,
Who's Bad . . .

(Black Bank Robber trying his best to moon walk - Dan starts shooting at his feet! I'm bad I'm Bad......] All the bank guest are clapping their hands. Dan gets carried away and shoots the gun up in the 3 mores times. Security guards rush to cuff the bank robbers as police show up from the activated silent alarm. Security guard removes the gun from Dan's hand.)

[FADES TO BLACK]

CHAPTER EIGHT

FOREIGN MILITARY RECRUITING

(EXT DAY. DAN'S HOUSE 103 CALUMENT ST - EARLY MORNING FRONT PORCH) [After a long time out of the scene Nicky appears at Dan's house to drop off a double wrapped brown manila envelope. He rings the doorbell. He rings the doorbell again.]

STEPHANIE [AS IF AWOKEN FROM HER SLEEP]

What? Who is it? Oh Nicky! Boy we haven't seen you in a long time. Did you fall off the face of earth?

NICKY

Hi Stephanie. How are you? Yes it has been a long time. I have been away working on my future. By the way is Dan home? I have just a few minutes and I want to give him something.

[Car horn honks as Nicky's friends are yelling at him to hurry up]

STEPHANIE

No Dan's not here. Do you want to come in for a minute?

NICKY

No No I really have to get going. Could you please give this package to Dan? It is very important. Please don't open it just give it to him as soon as possible. Promise?

STEPHANIE

Okay okay. Why doesn't anyone get me a package? I deserve something ya know.

NICKY

Stephanie do you promise? Its really important that he gets this right away.

STEPHANIE

Okay okay. I will. Now go so I can finish getting my beauty sleep.

(EXT DAY. DAN'S HOUSE 103 CALUMENT ST - AFTERNOON FRONT PORCH) [After the Bank scene Dan arrives home unaware the Nicky stopped by and dropped off the package. He is still upset about Stephanie telling the recruiters he was not interested in enlisting. He runs up the stairs and into the house.]

DAN

STEPHANIE! STEPHANIE! Where are you? Are you still sleeping?

STEPHANIE
Here I am. Whats up?

DAN
What's with you? What do you think you are doing with that stunt you pulled?

STEPHANIE
What stunt?

DAN
You telling the recruiters that I am not interested! And then telling me they never came! What the hell is wrong with you? My life is on hold! I tried to join the Army Green Berets, Navy SEALS - rejected!!! Rejected for life!! Okay so I am deaf! Just a little fricking deaf and it keeps me off the state police force, the metropolitan police force, the Boston police! I can't even get into the FRENCH FOREIGN LEGIONS [FLASH TO THE FFL INTERVIEW]

FRENCH FOREIGN RECRUITER (TO DAN)
Please place the cap on your head and walk across the room.

DAN

Okay now what?

DAN
I see ……

FRENCH FOREIGN RECRUITER (TO DAN)
Boom!!

DAN
What?

FRENCH FOREIGN RECRUITER (TO DAN)
Boom!!

DAN
What?

FRENCH FOREIGN RECRUITER (TO DAN)
Just as I thought. Whenever I say "boom!" you say "what"……If it were are real explosion or war you would say "what"… sorry you cannot join the Legion. I cannot.

[FLASH BACK TO CONVERSATION WITH STEPHANIE]

DAN
You know I can jump over a parked cars, I can climb mountains, hang from cliffs, I am an expert shooter and can shoot the head out of a quarter at 200 yards. There are many patriots in this country, fortunately, and many forms of patriotism.

Hopefully one day my patriotism will rest in the conduct of deeds, some requiring great personal courage, maybe to free hostages and to fight communism. But there's another form of patriotism which is unique to democracy. It resides in those who have a deep respect for the rule of law and faith in America's democratic traditions. To uphold our Constitution requires not the exceptional efforts of the few but the confidence and the trust and the work of the many.

Democracy has its frustrations. Capitalism is not perfect but its better than socialism and communism. Right now there is no better system of government in the United States except for having too many cooks in the kitchen at the same time.

STEPHANIE
What do you mean "cooks in the kitchen"?

DAN
That means when the United States Congress has agrees then disagrees during wartime or when there is a need to support a revolutionary movement i.e. freedom fighters "they" the Congress either takes too long to decide or changes their mind it people's lives are lost while we the USA claims - were gonna back you up—don't worry be happy. And then the support comes to late or not at all.

STEPHANIE
Oh (under her breath)

DAN
What? What did you say?

STEPHANIE
I just said oh.[Stephanie rolls her eyes and walks away - point being is that Dan cannot hear]

DAN
GET BACK HERE!!! DID I TELL YOU THAT I AM OUTTA HERE! YEP THAT'S RIGHT I AM GONE!!

STEPHANIE
NO! NO! Please please don't go….

[Dan is trying to leave the bedroom. Stephanie stands in front Dan blocking the bedroom door. Dan steps to the right, Stephanie steps to the right, Dan steps to the left, Stephanie steps to the left. Dan grabs Stephanie and picks her up. Her legs wrap around his waist.]

[Music by PINK fades in]

"Please Don't Leave Me"

Da da da da
Da da da da

Da da da da da,

I don't know if I can yell any louder,
How many times have I kicked you out of here
Or said something insulting?

Da da da da da

I can be so mean when I wanna be,
I am capable of really anything,
I can cut you into pieces,

DAN [TO STEPHANIE]
Now while I have your attention I have a personal question to ask you. Did you spill to tea on my favorite beige chair?

STEPHANIE
It's a pink chair!

DAN
It's a beige chair!

STEPHANIE
PINK!

DAN
BEIGE!

[Just then the doorbell rings]

DAN [TO STEPHANIE]
Who could that be? You stay here. Don't come out of the room.

STEPHANIE
No I wanna see who it is…..

DAN [TO STEPHANIE]
Why don't you ever listen? Nobody is coming here for you. Just wait until I am done

[buzz buzz door bell is ringing. Dan is walking quickly from the bedroom, down the hall, opens the hall door, gets to the front door. It Babe and the guys]

BABE
Dan whatz up whatz up?

DAN
Guys howz it going? Come on in come on i

BABE
I want to be the first to tell you that we got our orders for Boot Camp

DAN
Really now and you are eating ice cream? Shouldn't be trying to get in shape? When do you go?

BABE
Believe it or not Thanksgiving Day we get on the bus. Now that you mentioned it - can you get rid of the ice cream I'm and done with it. So we are having a farewell and we want you to come. You can bring whatz-her-face Stephanie to the Farewell. Its going to be at Dave Viola's house Thanksgiving day. His mom is a good cook.

[Dan takes the vanilla ice cream cone from Babe and opens the bedroom door ever so slightly. The cone is in his left hand - Stephanie is tied upside down to the door. Her mouth is gagged. Dan puts the ice cream in her crotch. It begins to slowly drip.]

[Camera zooms to Stephanie's eyes as Dan places the cold ice cream on her]

DAN
Well guys congratulations. I didn't get mine. So you probably will be leaving without me.

BABE
Don't worry Dan it will come thru. We will stick with you. Let us know if you need anything. Okay take care.

DAN
Okay guys take care.[Sadly Dan closes the front door]

CHAPTER NINE

HAPPY THANKSGIVING AND FAREWELL

(EXT. DAY - DAVE V'S HOUSE - THANKSGIVING DAY – 1:00PM)

[Stephanie and Dan walk up the drive at Dave's house and enter the Dining room where all Dan's friends are about to begin eating. Mrs. Viola welcomes Dan and Steph and tells them to sit down and get ready to eat.] [Table is full with traditional servings for thanksgiving a bit overboard]

DAVE V

Hey welcome to my humble abode. Dan you know the guys. For those of you who don't know this Dan's mother Stephanie. Okay okay just kidding. Okay now here is another fact: Have you've heard the myth that Ben Franklin wanted the turkey, not the bald eagle, to be the symbol of America. And, sure, turkey meat does make you sleepy. Turkey meat has more protein per ounce than nearly any other meat. A 3.5-ounce serving of turkey breast has 30 grams of protein, almost as much as beef (with 36 grams). In comparison, pork loin has only 25 grams, tuna and salmon 26 grams. There's a reason domesticated turkey meat has so little dark meat—dark meat is muscle tissue that stores oxygen in order to maximize efficiency for frequent use. Domesticated turkeys rarely fly (wild turkeys can fly short distances), so their breast muscles are underused. That's why wild turkey has a lot more dark meat than farm turkey does.

Did you know that the flap of red flesh on the top of a male turkey's beak is called a snood, which is interesting enough. But the really fascinating thing about the snood is that female turkeys (or hens or jennies) prefer to mate with males with longer snoods. The same goes for male turkeys (or toms or jakes) looking for some male-bonding time—they, too, prefer to hang out with longer-snooded toms. The reason may be that turkeys with longer snoods tend to have higher resistance to certain infections.
Ebenezer Scrooge sent a turkey, not a goose, to the Cratchits for Christmas dinner in *A Christmas Carol*. It strikes some folks as odd, given that this is a North American bird and the story came out in 1843. But turkeys had already become available in England by this time, supplanting traditional European holiday meats like pheasant and goose.

DAVE V'S DAD

Okay David enough with the Thanksgiving facts. You guys need to eat up so you don't miss the Marine bus today.

DAVE V

And Nooooooooo, tryptophan doesn't make you sleepy. Eating a lot does. It's called a food coma!

[And the FAREWELL Thanksgiving meal is served. Sun is shining through the window. Stephanie and Dan keep making eye contact sitting across from each other at the dining room table as the chatter continues in the room. Scene - fades away to Dan and Stephanie hand-in-hand skipping in a field all lovey duvey and music fades in: Nothing but Flowers]

"(Nothing But) Flowers"

Here we stand
Like an Adam and an Eve
Waterfalls
The Garden of Eden
Two fools in love
So beautiful and strong
The birds in the trees
Are smiling upon them
From the age of the dinosaurs
Cars have run on gasoline
Where, where have they gone?
Now, it's nothing but flowers

There was a factory
Now there are mountains and rivers
you got it, you got it

[Passed out on Mrs. V's couch and still in the middle of his dream (although in the dream Stephanie has been swapped out for Sophia Vergara) all Dan's friends, Dave's mom and dad are standing around watching Dan.]

[optional scene: various hits from the 1980 play while girls in fantasy keep changing every second]

[Dan is kissing and making mouth gestures still in his dream state. He is about to kiss his new fantasy Sophia Vergara just when Stephanie wakes him up].

STEPHANIE
Dan, Dan, Dan wake up. Wake up honey we have to go.

DAN
No, no, no, -- oh I thought you were someone else.

[group clapping at Dan's performance.]

DAVE V

Okay guys we got to get going. We have to get on that bus today

[All the guys pick up their knapsacks and make their way outside. They say their farewells. Each guy gives Dan a hug. "we won't forget you Dan. The USMC van stops and picks all Dan's friends (taking them the bus)]

STEPHANIE

Don't be sad Dan. I have something for you in my bag.

[Stephanie walks to the van and retrieve the double wrapped brown bag that Nicky dropped off]

STEPHANIE
Here this is from your invisible friend Nicky.

DAN
Well how did you get it?

STEPHANIE
Oh he gave it to me two weeks ago and said give it to you asap.

DAN
ASAP! (Gasping! -- Glaring/staring)ITS ALL GOING TO GET BETTER IN A MINUTE (

STEPHANIE
Yea! ASAP! I don't know what the hell the military terminology means. Anyway enjoy.

DAN
Okay okay what do we have here?

[Dan unwraps the package and drops the paper wrap to the ground. Trying to read as a fast as he can. It is orders to show up for an onsite visit at a secret training camp. Because Stephanie gave him the package so late everything in now urgent because he has just to days to show up.]

DAN
I gotta go. I gotta go. This is my golden opportunity.

STEPHANIE
Go where? You're not going anywhere without me buster!

DAN
Road trip.

CHAPTER TEN

TAKE OUT THE NEADTHERDAL

(EXT DAY. STEPHANIE'S HOUSE - NOON)

[Day of departure. Dan drives to Stephanie's house in West Roxbury to pick her up. Parks his van and walks up to the front door and rings the bell. Waits - rings the bell again. Thinking this is odd she usually answers fairly quick.](Moments later Stephanie opens the door somewhat out of breath and sweating.)

STEPHANIE
Hi! I didn't expect you so soon.

DAN
Well you do want to go on this trip with me right?

STEPHANIE
Oh yes! Wouldn't miss it for the world. Can you do me a favor? Can you go to the store and get me some juice for the trip?

DAN
Well can you let me use the bathroom first I have to go pee?

STEPHANIE
Oh okay

[Stephanie opens the door and they begin walking upstairs to the second level. Dan appears to walk toward the bathroom and Stephanie goes to her room and slams the door. Dan makes a 360 turn toward her door].

DAN
HEY OPEN UP!

STEPHANIE
No my room is a mess!

DAN
Come on open up I know you are a slob.

STEPHANIE
No really just go to the store for me.

[A bit suspicious of her behavior - Dan gets in his van and goes around the block and comes back to Stephanie's street and parks.][All of a sudden the front door of Stephanie's house opens. This brown haired 7 foot tall giant runs out of the house. As he gets out of the front yard and runs towards his car Dan jumps out of his van just up the street and starts yelling]

DAN [RUNNING TOWARD THE GIANT]

HEY YOU! STOP! STOP! YOU FRIGGIN NEANDTHERAL!!!!!!!

(The giant takes off in his blue hyped up cutlass supreme. Laughing like a maniac Dan runs back to his van and the chase begins] Mumbling out loud - this giant is going to kick my azz. Dan unzips a gym bag and begins stuffing socks and underwear into his sweatshirt to appear muscular. With ablue magic marker Dan makes a tattoo and writes "killer" on his neck)

(After driving from West Roxbury to Mattapan the giant is stuck at a red light. Dan jumps out of his van and jumps up and down on the giant's trunk, roof - Imitating the HULK Dan jumps on the hood facing the giant- then jumps off and kicks the front bumper setting of the airbag and knocks out the giant. Dan jumps in his van and drives away.)

TALKING HEADS
"Psycho Killer"

I can't seem to face up to the facts
I'm tense and nervous and I
Can't relax
I can't sleep 'cause my bed's on fire
Don't touch me I'm a real live wire

CHAPTER ELEVEN

ROAD TRIP TO CAMP PEARY

(EXT. DAN RETURNS TO STEPHANIE'S HOUSE NEXT DAY- VANISHING POINT VAN – 1:00PM)

DAN

[Rings the bell] What the hell was that? I show up to pick up my girlfriend to go on a trip and a frigging yellow ape NEADERTHAL comes running out the front door!!

STEPHANIE

I was just doing a massage trying to make money for the trip. Please don't be mad honey. I was doing it for usssss.

DAN

Yeah RIGHT! And I was born last Tuesday. Look I have a lot of pressure right now. I have to get going. I am going to forget about the Neanderthal ape so let's get out of here. This is the beginning of our road trip and there are a few rules you need to agree to - ok?

STEPHANIE

Oh sure like what?

DAN

No open cans of juice. I don't want anything spilling. All food must be put in the fridge. Keep nothing out that is going to smell or spoil. If we get stopped for speeding you are not to say anything to the police. Got it!

STEPHANIE
Okay got it!

DAN
Promise?

STEPHANIE
Promise!

[Dan turns on the radio. An early snowstorm is on the way. To avoid the snow coming from the north Dan gets on the Jamaica-way (fast road near Boston) before the highway.]

[RADIO: We interrupt this broadcast to announce a winter storm warning is in effect for the New England area. The storm is headed to the northeast and snow will be heavy at times]

[10 minutes into the road trip police flip on the siren and lights. Dan pulls over (now raining very hard) to avoid getting a ticket - Dan goes into character as paraplegic scientist Stephen Hawkins.]

POLICE OFFICER
License and registration please.

DAN (IMITATING STEPHEN HAWKINS/STUTTERING)
O o o o o o kay Oooooo Officer one one one moment please. I I I I I I I aayyyyyyyyyyyayy will get it for you.

[Both Stephanie and the officer were taken by surprised when Dan began acting.]

[Dan and Stephanie whisper bickering]

DAN [TO STEPHANIE QUIETLY]
Where the hell is my registration? Come on look in the pouch he is getting soaking wet. I don't want to piss him off.

STEPHANIE [TO DAN QUIETLY]
What is with the I,I,I,I,I, you sound like a broken record - whose does that?

[The officer is standing in the sleet rain waiting. Dan feels bad the officer is getting wet so he is frantically looking for his license and registration.]

POLICE OFFICER
[Getting impatient] Do YOU KNOW WHY I PULLED YOU OVER???

DAN (AS STEPHEN HAWKINGS)

I I I I I I I I I I I I

STEPHANIE
[Stephanie leans over Dan] Officer we are trying to get to Virginia before the snow storm comes!

[The officer hands Dan the ticket and yells. Walks back to his car and leaves]

POLICE OFFICER
SLOW IT DOWN!!!!

DAN (TO STEPHANIE)
Did I tell you not to say anything.

[First stop is Virginia]

EXT DAY – ROAD TRIP DRIVING PASS THE WELCOME SIGNS (MUSIC-TALKING HEADS ROAD TO NO WHERE)

© Can Stock Photo - csp17829586

DAN [reading the signs]
The police cannot use radar detectors - coooool!

[Dan and Stephanie arrives at a government bus stop. Dan [rushing] kisses Stephanie goodbye and throws his back pack over his shoulder. Exits the van and gets in line to board the bus. From the manila envelope he hands the pass to the greeter and boards the bus.
About 20 other recruits are onboard. No one talks and the bus pulls away. Stephanie waves out the window and Dan doesn't wave back.

As the bus drives on they eventually pass Arlington National Cemetery. In {silence} Dan stands up and holds a salute while the other recruits notice. They too all stand in silence saluting until the bus passes the final grave stones. All you could hear was the bus engines.
Dan says out loud I hope to be BURIED IN ARLINGTON NATIONAL CEMENTARY one day............

[The bus comes to a stop at CIA/HQ and recruits disembark]

[Greeter hands out badges and asked everyone to sign in]

[Agent welcomes group yada yada yda]

[NOTE: YOU MUST CONTACT THE WRITER TO ENSURE THIS SECTION IS UPDATED WITH DECLASSIFIED SECTION]

CLASSIFIED

[POLYGRAPH STORY JUMPS TO TRAVEL TO CAMP PEARY]
[3 days of polygraphing]

[Visual - pass the sign on the highway "Eat more Chicken"]

[MUSIC BY TALKING HEADS]
"LIFE DURING WAR TIME"

Heard of a van that is loaded with weapons,
packed up and ready to go
Heard of some gravesites, out by the highway,
a place where nobody knows
The sound of gunfire, off in the distance,
I'm getting used to it now
Lived in a brownstore, lived in the ghetto,
I've lived all over this town

This ain't no party, this ain't no disco,
this ain't no fooling around
No time for dancing, or lovey dovey,
I ain't got time for that now

[FADE TO BLACK]

EXT. DAY HIGHWAY

[ROAD SIGN: Welcome to Williamsburg VA]

[Dan and Stephanie arrives at motel just a short drive from Camp Peary.

DAN

[After checking in] Stephanie I have to go to my training at the camp. I am going to be gone for two weeks. Please find something to do to keep yourself busy until I get back.

STEPHANIE

[Twurling and playing with her long hair] Do you really have to go? I don't want to be alone.

DAN

[Kissing her on the forehead] You know this is important to me. Please hang in there and wish me luck. If I don't make this I have no idea what I will do with my life - and then where will we be? Good bye for now.

[STEPHANIE WAITING FOR ME WHILE I AM IN CAMP PEARY TRAINING]

(Dan gets in his van and drives to the gate at Camp Peary. His eyes scan the entrance area and notices all the security cameras.)

GUARD
Sir may I help you?

DAN
(Handing the Guard the brown envelop) Yes I have an appointment.

(Dan whispering to himself)-- This must be the place. Yessssss I am hommmmmeeeeeeeee!

(Guard hands Dan a pass and opens the gate. Every few feet on the road is a white gloved guard (face covered) waving Dan on to the next intersection. Then suddenly there were no more guards giving direction.)

(SONG FADES IN) DAN CONTINUES DRIVING AROUND CAMP PEARY)

"This Must Be The Place (Naive Melody)"

Home is where I want to be
Pick me up and turn me round
I feel numb - born with a weak heart
I guess I must be having fun
The less we say about it the better
Make it up as we go along
Feet on the ground
Head in the sky
It's ok I know nothing's wrong... nothing

Hi yo I got plenty of time
Hi yo you got light in your eyes
And you're standing here beside me
I love the passing of time
Never for money
Always for love
Cover up and say goodnight... say good night

[SIGN - ARMED FORCES EXPERIMENTAL TRAINING ACTIVITY A.F.E.T.A.]

[Visuals inside the camp next to airport runway)

(Dan parks his van, gets out and walks toward the building. A masked guard points to Dan to get in line. There are others already here waiting. No conversation and no eye contact. We are all just waiting. Just then a man with a clip board appears- the greeter.)

NARRATOR V.O

And now comes the time to learn, learn, learn politics, the good guys, the bad guys, the Idi Amin dada types, the Khaddafis, and Pinoches,the Saudis friend and foe alike. Each recruit will improve and develop their skills…….very very fast as well as learn some pretty neat tricks!

(SONG CONTINUES IN THE BACKGROUND) **GREETER**

Sorry for the delay. Please get in a single file and hand me the card that you received from the guard at the front gate. I will be handing out a pass with the building code. Read it and gather your things then walk inside to the conference hall.

(SONG CONTINUES IN THE BACKGROUND THEN FADES)

[THE GREETER IS A SHORT GUY [LOOKS LIKE A FIRE PLUG]THAT HAS A HITLER MUSTACH ON HIS CHIN. HE IS KNOWN FOR STARTING OFF KIND AND SWEET THEN TURNING INTO A RANT - LIKE HITLER. AFTER HE SPEAKS AND BEHIND HIS BACK HE GETS SALUTED BY THE SMART ASSES IN THE CROWD - HEIL HITLER]

GREETER

(WALKS UP THE STEPS TO THE STAGE PODIUM TO GREET THE CLASS OF 50 RECRUITS)

Welcome to Camp Peary - aka The FARM. We have a lot of work to do over the next 2 weeks before we ship you off to Ft. Benning School of the Americas.

It is my pleasure to welcome you to this fine institution that is nowhere on any map. You the few have been chosen because of your unique type A personalities, a leader. A person with charisma and confidence. A person with special or unique skills. We all have basic human needs, but as personalities or characters we have desires and real-life roles to play. It is therefore essential to pinpoint personality and character traits when evaluating a person or scanning a crowd. The easiest way to do this in a crowd setting is of course through observation of body language.

Con-Artists and Agents look specifically for these personality types, keeping in mind that people are complex and dynamic beings and these generalized personality types do not always apply but they are still useful for most practical purposes.

The essential game being played is a match-making game. Find out who that person is, and make yourself their match. The match can be complimentary or an offset, it varies with the personality type. Everyone has their weakness. Your job is to find it and figure out a way to exploit it.

[Greeter drones on and on - recruits are starting to fall asleep in their seats]

Out in the field there is a desire to please others - These people are looking for someone to please, and are the easiest to manipulate if you know how to approach them correctly. First it requires a Type A personality, a leader. This person is looking for charisma and confidence. Your opinion matters to them, and the more important you appear, the more important your opinion will be to them. This personality type is passive and would prefer not to make decisions. They are often attracted to others who can make the decisions for them, they do not like giving their opinions of things for fear of being wrong and drawing scorn.

[Greeter pulls out his gun and fires X3 up in the air - scaring the kahoonas out of everyone]

GREETER's GUN

Blam! Blam! Blam!

[Recruits that have martial arts jump up into a kung fu pose while others fall off their seats]

GREETER

We can always tell who holds a black belt when I do that…. So as I was saying in the name of national security we want to know these people inside and out. We want to be three steps ahead of decision makers. It is up to you to gain access to world decision makers and report back. Always continue to improve upon your craft….since we don't use names here each of you will have an assigned number. Tell anyone your name and you will be out.

[all recruits are clapping]

GREETER

Get some sleep we have a busy schedule tomorrow. You will have to report to MED that is medical evaluation to be sure you have the cognitive, physical and sensory requirements to be here!!!

(All recruits pick up their items and begin to move out of the great hall.)

EXT. - EARLY MORNING CAMP PEARY DORM/BARRACKS

(Dan is headed to MED. There is a line ahead of him. Each recruit must enter 1 of 6 wooden doors. All others await outside on wooden benches in the MED building lobby)

[Music fades in and remains on low volume as camera shows each recruit x6 entering the room to sit down on the about to undergo questions and examination from various old and young medical doctors. Some questions are rapid fire as camera jumps from recruit to recruit's facial expressions)

[TALKING HEADS BACKGROUND MUSIC] "Slippery People"

What about the time?
You were rollin' over
Fall on your face
You must be having fun
Walk lightly!
Think of a time.
You'd best believe
This think is real

Put away that gun
This part is simple
Try to recognize
What is in you mind
God help us!
Help us loose our minds
These slippery people
help us understand

what's the matter with him? He's alright!
I see his face The lord won't mind
Don't play no games He's alright
Love from the bottom to the top
Turn like a wheel He's alright
See for yourself The lord won't mind
We're gonna move Right now
Turn like a wheel inside a wheel

(While Slippery People music playing)

(FLASH) MED DOCTOR 1 (TO 1ST RECRUIT)
Did you ever climb a tree?

(FLASH) MED DOCTOR 2 (TO 2ND RECRUIT)
Did you ever climb a tree?

(FLASH) MED DOCTOR 3 (TO 3RD RECRUIT)
Did you ever climb a tree?

(FLASH) MED DOCTOR (TO RECRUIT)
Did you…….

(FLASH) MED DOCTOR 1 (TO RECRUIT)

Are you afraid of heights?

(FLASH) MED DOCTOR 2 (TO RECRUIT)

Are you willing to swallow cyanide if captured by the enemy?

(FLASH) AFRICAN AMERICAN RECRUIT

(Perplexed and confused because the recruit never heard of cyanide)Well sure but what does it taste like? Have you tasted it?

(FLASH {montage}To other recruits squatting and holding their ankles while trying to jump around the room - this is how their backs are checked for injury)

Shooters
VALET
PARKING

YOU CALL THIS A PARTY?
PFCRN
LOS COLONOS
DE SANTA MARTHA DEL SUR
"EXIJIMOS"
LOTIFICACION EN NUESTROS
TERRENOS Y APRUEBEN PROY
SI SOLUCION
NO AGRECION

USA

[AT THE RANGE: Early morning Dan and a couple of recruits are at the range. One recruit is kneeling down, pulls the pin on the grenade and tosses to another recruit who hits it with a bat sending it to the outfield where it explodes. While this is going on another guy walks up and purchases 3 grenades]

DAN (TO GRENADE SELLER)
Who was that guy?

GRENADE SELLER
Oh he is the landscaper. He uses grenades to blow up tree stumps.

DAN (TO GRENADE SELLER)
Yeah but you are selling government property…

GRENADE SELLER
I know but its government trees…

[FADE TO BLACK]

INT. - EVENING CAMP PEARY DORM/BARRACKS

(SPECIAL SKILLS DISCUSSION)

(Dan reading his itinerary begins walking down the dorm hallway. Dan strikes up a conversation with the guy walking next to him. Dan learns that this guy is going to be Accelerated CNX program. He is also designated sharpshooter and has the same background as Dan. In just a short time Dan finds out about several other recruits in his group that are in the Remote Viewing and ESP CIA programs.)

DAN (TO AGENT IN TRAINING IN DIRECTOR'S WAITING ROOM)

Hi how are you? My name is Mr. 46857.

AGENT IN TRAINING

[reaching out to shake hands] Mike, Mike Costello. Pleasure to meet you. Are you in the CNX program?

DAN (TO AGENT IN TRAINING IN DIRECTOR'S WAITING ROOM)

Oh I am not sure yet but things are progressing fast.

AGENT IN TRAINING (BRAGGING)Yes - the CNX is a faster much more accelerated than typical training for an intelligence agent includes but is not limited to: covert surveillance, slight of hand, con-artistry, manipulation tactics, personality-type identification, lying, cheating, stealing, trickery, camouflage, evasion, escape, improvised weaponry, improvised self-defense, analytical combat, and espionage. Part of intelligence training is instruction in something called the "Dark Arts". The Dark Arts are the espionage, trickery, con artistry type stuff. And then there is the weird ones like Remote Viewing like ESP and Mind Control for Dummies. The study shows some proof to human precognition -- at least when it comes to porn. Its not like being back on the block once your in - *your in.*

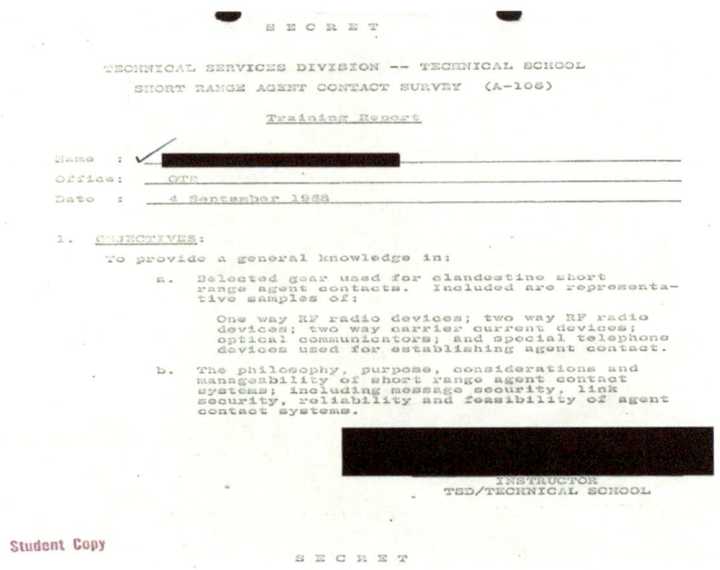

S E C R E T

TECHNICAL SERVICES DIVISION -- TECHNICAL SCHOOL
SHORT RANGE AGENT CONTACT SURVEY (A-106)

Training Report

Name : [redacted]
Office: OTR
Date : 4 September 1968

1. OBJECTIVES:

To provide a general knowledge in:

a. Selected gear used for clandestine short range agent contacts. Included are representative samples of:

One way RF radio devices; two way RF radio devices; two way carrier current devices; optical communicators; and special telephone devices used for establishing agent contact.

b. The philosophy, purpose, considerations and manageability of short range agent contact systems; including message security, link security, reliability and feasibility of agent contact systems.

INSTRUCTOR
TSD/TECHNICAL SCHOOL

Student Copy

S E C R E T

(SIGN ON DIRECTOR'S DOOR)

Ye shall know the truth and it shall set you free."

DAN (TO AGENT IN TRAINING IN DIRECTOR'S WAITING ROOM)

Oh yes yes of course the "Dark Arts". The Dark Arts are the espionage, trickery, con artistry type stuff. Not everyone has what it takes to effectively pull this off. It takes confidence and a good amount of acting. It takes an artist who is quick, versatile, and creative. But if studied, practiced, and perfected these methods can and do work.

DESK OFFICER (LOUDLY)

46857 REPORT TO ROOM 4301 COSTELLO REPORT TO ROOM 435

(Dan enters the room and sees a parrot in a cage.)

PARROT

I'm cool!

DAN

No ya not. I'm cool!

PARROT

I'm cool!

DAN

I'm cool!

PARROT

I'm cooler than you!

DAN

Ha! I'm way cooler than you!

PARROT

I can talk but can you fly?

(Just then the office door opens and a curvy hot secretary walks in)

SECERTARY

Oh I see you've met Woodyee.

DAN

YeP AND I am still cooler than him.

PARROT

Hey get me a drink! I am waiting for a drink all dayyyyyyy. And YOU (to Dan) I am way cooler than you'll ever be. WHERE IS MY DRINK that I ORDERED!!!!!!

[Mike and Dan get up at the same time. Mike gives Dan a shoulder hug as they were longtime friends. Dan hijacks Mike's orders to find out if they have a better program than his. Dan is reading Mike's orders as fast as he can walking down the hall toward the Training Coordinator's office]

[When Dan arrives in the Training Coordinator's office by coincidence the Director of CN (counter-narcotics) Program is there using a remote control to change the TV news. A fly begins to irritate the Director so while he is focused on the TV he picks up a fly swatter.]

TRAINING COORDINATOR [EXTENDS HIS HAND TO DAN]

Welcome! Good to see you. Heard a lot of good things about you. Damn fly!!

DAN [TO TRAINING COORD]

Glad to be here! I am looking forward to the next step.

[Conversation interrupted as Training Director abruptly walks in looking for his TV remote control]

TRAINING DIRECTOR [TO TRAINING COORD]
Excuse me did you see the remote control anywhere? I could of sworn I had it with me when I was in here a while ago.

TRAINING COORD
Sir, no I haven't seen it in here. Sir, this is Mr. 46857 a new recruit

TRAINING DIRECTOR
Welcome! Good to see you. Heard a lot of good things about you. Can you look under that seat for the remote?

DAN [TO TRAINING DIRECTOR]
Excuse me sir? Whats a remote?

TRAINING DIRECTOR
Whats a remote? Come on son your fooling me. A TV remote control is one of the most amazing things ever invented.

DAN [TO TRAINING DIRECTOR]

[searching the sofa pillows] Sir is this it?

TRAINING DIRECTOR
Yes that's it! This is the most popular remote control called Starcom of Jerrold which uses 40-kHz sound to change TV channels. It comes with a Viewstar converter -----an immediate success, the millionth converter being sold on March 21, 1985. Anyone takes my TV remote I swear I won't kill them but I will make 'em disappear. Thanks for finding it for me.

[Facing away Dan using his ventriloquism he puts words in the director's mouth "I want Dan Sin in the Accelerated CNX814 program" and the Training Coordinator responds]

TRAINING COORD
Yes Sir! Absolutely

TRAINING DIRECTOR
Huh?

TRAINING COORD
46857 take this to Psycho Testing and then over to Special Activities Division just across the yard. Look for the…. Bigler's Mill sign..

(Dan walks outside to get a breath of fresh air and takes in the small step of progress of his future. He begins to walk across camp. There is a commotion on the side of the building. A few recruits all kneeling down playing some game. So Dan stands there for a minute while the guys are playing and all of a sudden…..)

CAMP PEARY DRILL INSTRUCTOR
[sneaks up behind a recruit] [all stand up]

WHY ARE YOU GAMBLING BOY?

NEW RECRUIT
TO MAKE MONEY SIR!!

CAMP PEARY DRILL INSTRUCTOR
You don't have enough money boy?

NEW RECRUIT
No sir! Sir!

CAMP PEARY DRILL INSTRUCTOR [WARREN OATES TYPE]
You know boy I was so poor, so poor that I came home one night and the cockroaches left me a note - and DO YOU KNOW WHAT THAT NOTE FROM THE COCKROACHES SAID??????

NEW RECRUIT
NO SIR! NO IDEA WHAT THE NOTE FROM THE COCKROACHES SAID SIR!!

CAMP PEARY DRILL INSTRUCTOR
It said "wherezzz is all da the food at?" BUT YOU DON'T SEE ME GAMBLING OVER HERE DO YOU BOY????????

NEW RECRUIT
NO SIR!!!!   I DO NOT SIR!!!!

CAMP PEARY DRILL INSTRUCTOR
BOY -- YOUR PROBABLY SO POOR YOUR COCKROACHES ARE ON WELFARE!! NOW CLEAN THIS MESS UP AND GO DO SOMETHING INTELLIGENT WITH YOUR DOWN TIME!!!![all recruits scatter]

(RANGE 33)

(Day 13 at the Camp Peary Firing Range - Two SME are discussing Dan's superior eyesight the level of accuracy Dan is displaying at the range. Dan's shooter skills in each weapon are at the Sharpshooter Distinguished Expert: Aggregate course of fire shot five times with a score of 201/300 or better in each aggregate - and the instructors are noticing 275 RANKS HIGH)

(Dan is entering classroom - sign on the door DESIGNATED DEFENSIVE MARKSMAN (DDM) class is in progress. Dan opens the walks in and takes a seat in a class of 20 DDM trainees)

DDM INSTRUCTOR [TO CLASS]

Ok take a seat everyone. I asked you all to come up with group names so when we head over to the range we will break out into groups and we will use the same team names for the final competition - the names are:

THE SHOOTERS
THE KNOCKOUTS
THE WIDOWMAKERS
THE-SEE JOHNNY RUN RUN
THE CATACOMB CLUB
THE WE FIX STUFF MECHANICS
KELLY'S ASSASSINS
THE DEATH DO US PART
ZOMBIE MAKERS

DDM INSTRUCTOR [TO CLASS]

There are many things to know. Wind classification, wind velocity. How much effect will the wind have on the bullet? A common method of estimating velocity of the wind is to watch a flag. If no flag is visible use a piece of grass, cotton or some other light piece of material. All telescopic sights must have windage adjustments that are graduated in minutes of angle or fraction thereof.

UTILIZING THE TECHNIQUES TAUGHT, ZEROING AND FIELD EXPEDIENT ZERO WILL BOOST NOT ONLY YOUR CONFIDENCE IN YOUR WEAPON BUT WILL ASSIST IN MAKING SURE YOU RETURN FROM THE MISSION - ALIVE.

DDM INSTRUCTOR [TO CLASS]

[There is a knock on the classroom door-instructor walking to the door while talking to the class]

Class just one moment please - could Recruit 46857 show yourself?

VISITOR

Sir is there Recruit 46857 in your class? If so we need to speak with him.

DDM INSTRUCTOR [TO CLASS]
46857 - Fall out ……..

(Dan under his breath - okay now what?)

(Dan enters the hallway where he is greeted by two undercover agents in trench coats)

AGENT 1
46857?- you are 46857 correct?

(Agent is making Dan uncomfortable by staring at the sides of Dan's head to see his ears)

DAN
Yes I am he. What can I do for you?

AGENT 2
46857 we heard a lot of good things about you. We also found in your file that you are hearing impaired. Do you use sign language or lip read?

DAN
Well I lip read. I have never had sign language training since I've always been in regular schools with kids that could hear -- why?

AGENT 2
Reads lips - good![checking the box in paper on clip board]

AGENT 1

46857 in your folder it states that you have had a lot of training with firearms and you are in good physical condition. Are you? Can you read lips using binoculars and or sniper scope?

DAN
Yes that's true and yes I can.

AGENT 2
After your training we have a mission for you. If you accept the mission you know the deal. No one knows. And we don't know you.

DAN
And you said your name was????

AGENT 2
I didn't say BUT I am Mike and he is Donovan. We are scouts for Delta Force. We review all the recruit files to find unique and special talent among the ranks. We want to use your lip reading skills down range. We have a requirement for a lip

reader with sniper skills. After your training we will introduce downrange Delta Commandos who reside at Fort Bragg North Carolina. We understand that you will be headed for training at the School of Americas in Fort Benning Georgia. Perhaps you can rondevu with Delta Special Ops at Ft. Benning. We'll be in touch

DAN

[under his breath] lip reading sniper - yep that'd be me… It's all gonna get better in a minute.

[FADE TO BLACK]

NIGHT TIME AT THE RANGE

RADAR

[Out of breath from running] Capt Hunnicutt, Capt Hunnicutt 46857 is gambling down at the range.

CAPT HUNNICUTT

[Placing hand on Radar's shoulder] Radar, Radar take it easy… breath take a deep breath. Now tell me whats going on?

RADAR

Well Sir 46857 and a couple of operators were headed over to the range and from what I understand sir they a betting on hitting targets. And you sir specifically said no gambling was allow while you are in charge.

CAPT HUNNICUTT

[Slapping Radar on the back] Alright Radar lets head over to the range and find out what's going on.

As Radar and Capt Hunnicutt approach the dimly lit outdoor range they see a group of recruits standing around 46857. As Capt Hunnicutt approaches they all stand at attention.

CAPT HUNNICUTT

[Loudly] Alright at ease. 46857 I hear you are running some kind of scam.

SHEA/46857

No sir no scam sir just some honest God good ole American gambling sir. I bet that I can shoot the head out of a 50 cent piece at what length one can throw.

CAPT HUNNICUTT

Okay 46857 you have captured my interest. One of you guys bet him and lets see what he's got?

NEW RECRUIT
[Loudly] ok ok I bet 5 dollars 46857 can't hit this silver dollar. Are you ready?

SHEA/46857
[Loudly] Anytime I am ready….

NEW RECRUIT
[Loudly] ok 1, 2, 3

SHEA/46857
[BAM! SHEA FIRES OFF A ROUND]
Okay go get it.

New recruit picks up the silver dollar and walks over to show Hunnicutt.

CAPT HUNNICUTT
Wow 46857 you have some skill there… Now lets see if you can shoot 5 silver dollars at the same time? Will you take that bet for $100 bucks? Can you do it?

SHEA/46857
Yes Sir I will give it my best shot.

Everyone is excited to see if he can make the shot.

FLASH TO END OF RANGE OUT OF SIGHT: In the bush you see 5 Special Operators friends of 46857 wearing night vision optics talking to each other.

SPECIAL OPERATOR/1
[BAM! SHEA FIRES IN SYNC WITH OTHER OPERATORS] Remind me again why 46857 needs 5 of us out here?

SPECIAL OPERATOR/2
46857 said that 5 is the maximum number of coins to shoot..

SHEA/46857
[BAM! BAM! BAM! BAM! BAM! SHEA FIRES OFF 5 ROUNDs] Okay go get it.

New recruit picks up the 5 silver dollar and walks over to show Hunnicutt.

CAPT HUNNICUTT
Wow 46857 THAT'S AMAZING!
Where did you learn to shoot like that?

SHEA/46857
Well Sir when I spent some time in Texas there was this place called the Grassy Knoll.

CAPT HUNNICUTT
Really Really good I must say. Lets everyone head of to the Watering Hole they having the annual contest tonight. Should be good.

[EXT - AFTERNOON CAMP PEARY WATERING HOLE TALENT SHOW (CPWHTS]
[UPLIGHTS-BAR SCENE STAGE AND PATRONS]

Guy on the Mic
WELCOME TO THE CAMP PEARY WATERING HOLE
SOME OF YOU COME HERE TO LEARN SKILLS AND SOME OF YOU BRING WITH YOU AMAZING TRICKS AND TIPS TO BE USED IN THE FIELD-SHOW US YOUR TALENT!!

Ok lets open this up - we want folks to tell us who they are, talent if they have one, and what the hope and wish for........
And for all you E.D.P.(s) Emotionally Disturbed People - [Stare into the camera]and no the government hasn't installed a microchip in your brain. YOU ARE NOT THAT IMPORTANT!!!
Okay okay whoooooo is first up ACT 1?

[Sitting across the a hand goes up]

Guy on the Mic
Ok let's welcome our first sucker I mean gentleman and you are???

Tony
My name is Tony but my friends call me Lenny

Guy on the Mic
And what do you do Lenny?

Tony
Are you a friend of mine? You just called me Lenny?

Guy on the Mic
Ummm umm okay what do you prefer…
Tony
Call me Joeseppi [audience laughs]
Guy on the Mic
And what do you do Joeseppi?
LENNY [Italian accent]

[Lenny just stares for a moment]
If I told you then I would have to kill you….

Guy on the Mic
No I mean what are your talents and where are you from?
LENNY
Well obviously I am from Italy but I came here from the Bronx….and I fix things. I am a fixer.

Guy on the Mic
You fix things? Like broken things?
LENNY
Yeah you could say that and sometimes I break things that have to be fixed. Ya know what I mean heh heh..
Guy on the Mic
[Nervously] Okay so what are you going to do today Joeseppi….?
LENNY
I need a person from the audience (soldier stands up). Okay now I don't know you. We never met before? (soldier shaking his head no] Well I have been practicing this card trick. (pulls out a deck of cards) Pick a card, any card, and show it to the audience.

Guy on the Mic
[Nervously] Okay audience check it out….[shows the audience][soldier showing card]
LENNY
Hmmmm (squinting his eyes) hmmmm it is… 8 of spades?????
AUDIENCE
bbbOOOOOOO(HECKLER - GET RID OF THE BUM!!)

Guy on the Mic
[Nervously] okay we are going for 2 out 2. Okay audience check it out….[shows the audience][soldier showing card]

LENNY
Okay okay one more time Hmmmm (squinting his eyes) hmmmm it is… jack of diamond?????
AUDIENCE
bbbOOOOOOO(HECKLER - GET RID OF THE BUM!!)

LENNY
Okay okay like I said I am new at this trick (begins to walk away)(soldier begins to sit down) oh before I forget (handing the soilder)here is your car keys…. And your gun….and your wallet.

AUDIENCE
Wow (clapping)hoot hoot hoot - go lennnny! go lennnnny! go lennnnnny! in sync.

LENNY
[to the audience] do I know you? Are you a friend of mine?

AUDIENCE
[CHANGES HIS NAME] Wow (clapping)hoot hoot hoot - go josepiiii! go josepiiii! go joeseppi! in sync.[clapping] all sit down.

Guy on the Mic
Well that wasn't that nice (imitating church lady SNL). Life is like a box of chocolates - you never know what you'll get. Let us turn our attention to ACT 2

Tiny Tim.

TINY TIM (LOOK ALIKE)

(On stage in a single stool strumming his ukulele)
I am tip toeing thru the tulips, tip toeing thru the tulips

[In acapella)
Tiptoe through the window
By the window, that is where I'll be
Come tiptoe through the tulips with me

Oh, tiptoe from the garden
By the garden of the willow tree
And tiptoe through the tulips with me

AUDIENCE

bbbOOOOOOO(HECKLER - GET RID OF THE BUM!!)

TINY TIM (Stands Up and aims his ukulele over the audiences' heads)

All together now….. Tiptoe through the tulips…[ukulele is a mini flame thrower with a huge flame]

Guy on the Mic

Okay that was our man on the street Tiny Tim. Don't worry folks it's all gonna get better in a minute - now lets welcome our next guest -
LOUDLY ---[TALKING HEADS MUSIC FADES IN: WILD WILD LIFE.]

-[FLASH TO MONTAGE:

ACT 3: KNIFE THROWER JUGGLERS ACT 4: NINJA ACROBATS
FLASH TO FAT RECRUIT ON THE FLOOR --- WHAT IS YOUR NAME????
ACT 5: FLASHING LIGHTS LIKE A FUNNY SOUL TRAIN LINE DANCE
FLASH TO FAT RECRUIT ON THE FLOOR - WHAT IS YOUR NAME ???
ACT 6: SNAKE GIRL IN THE SUITCASE]
FLASH TO FAT RECRUIT ON THE FLOOR - ITS JOHN CONNOR!!!
NO - ITS NOT…. THIS IS NOT TERMINATOR!! [PLACING DIFRIBRILLATORS ON HIS CHEST]BZZZZZZZ [SHOCKING THE RECRUIT] WHAT IS YOUR NAME?? JOHN CONNOR!!!
When shocking the recruit a second time he grabs the defibrillators and throws them into the mud wrestling pool. Two women light up being shocked and hit the floor of the 2 foot pool.

Other optional acts:
Pedro - (Spanish Godworshipping Genius)one leg fight simulation - beats the group with fake leg
Zoot -(Girl passing as GUY)pulls c4 grenades from vagina (everyone mouths I thought she was a guy.
Dillinger -(Genius Killer)loaded with hidden weapons
Einstein - (Genius TNT expert)

Old man - beats out young guy because he is a mind reader

[OLD MAN - FAT BELLY WALKS AWAY WITH TWO BIG BREASTED BABES UNDER EACH ARM. RECRUIT SAYS TO DAN - DID YOU SEE THAT (AS IN HOW DID THAT FAT GUY GET THE BABES?]
FAT GUY LOOKS OVER HIS SHOULD TOWARD DAN AND RECRUIT -POINTS TO HIS HEAD -- > AND SAYS ESP HA HA!!

(TBD) ACT: CAMP PEARY WATERING HOLE TALENT SHOW (CPWHTS] continues offstage near dart board wall:
[Naked Rubic Cube Game: Group of male recruits dare the female recruits (from another dorm) to play the NAKED RUBIC CUBE game. 5 girls compete with 5 guys. They

flip a coin to see who goes first. Girls call heads and guys get tails. Coin lands with tails up. Girls can spin/mess up the cube and the guys will have 30 seconds behind their backs to correctly restore the cube to solid colors. If the guys can do it in time the girls will have to take of an item of cloths.]

Guy on the Mic
Ok ladies step right up and tell us your names

Girls (talking into the mic)
I am Sheila, Kathy, Suzi, Andrea, and Betty

Guy on the Mic
Ok guys give the girls your cubes - and ladies mess them up!

Guy on the Mic
Ok girls had the guys the cubes and we will set the timer!!

Guy on the Mic
Get set.....[ding! Goes the bell]

[Background audience - together 1,2,3 Goooooo]

Guy on the Mic
Round 1 --And there off!!! - look at them goooooo They are working them like a monkey's uncle!! [in his best Howard Cosell impersonation]

Guy on the Mic
And they did it!!

[Guys holding up a completed rubics cube]

[Girls begin taking off something in slow motion. Really showing their assets by bending over etc]
[By round three the girls are down to underwear and bras (nice bodies)
[All of a sudden an unexpected female instructor shows up and blows her whistle - music stops - room goes silent]

SISTER C INSTRUCTOR [blowing her whistle]
Tweeeeeeeeeeeeeeeeeeeeettttttttttt

[Room goes silent all heads turn toward Sister C Instructor]

SISTER C INSTRUCTOR [blowing her whistle]
Holy mother of Mary. I have never seen in my life a bunch of grown women being duped into a childish game of strip rubic cube...... and you call yourself (pointing at the women) INTELLIGENCE PROFESSIONALS???????????????????

[ALL SILENT]

SISTER C INSTRUCTOR [Looking at big breasted Andrea]
Do you even know that these guys are duping you? Do you know that they each have a second completed cube making you think that they got it done in 30 seconds???? Nooooo they swapped them out!!!!

[each round an audience guy would hand a finished cube to the contestant guy appearing that he did it himself but really there were 10 cubes 5 done and 5 messed up]

ANDREA [TO SISTER C INSTRUCTOR]

Yes we knew they were duping us the whole time [pointing up to the mirrored ceiling/CAN CLEARLY SEE THE CHEATING]] But we just wanted to have funnnnn.

DAN [TO SISTER C INSTRUCTOR]

No way! Can't be! Is it you Sister C from my elementary school?

SISTER C INSTRUCTOR [Sitting down as if defeated after recognizing Dan]

Yes yes, I left the convent in search of a more forfilling career.

DAN [TO SISTER C INSTRUCTOR]

I am amazed! Who would ever thought…. On the outside you look great! On the inside you haven't changed a bit!!!!!

SISTER C INSTRUCTOR [Picking up a long ruler]

Okay okay!! Show is over! Everybody out!

[Begins to swing the ruler as if she had a flashback to school days] Fade to black…..
[Sister "C" Carolina's reinvents herself as Camp Peary Instructor]

[GRADUATION DAY - CAMP PEARY]

[**INT. DAY FADE IN - LARGE CEREMONY ROOM]**

CAMP COMMANDER [FINAL FAREWELL]

Three things to remember:

1. Try to look unimportant; the enemy may be low on ammo and not want to waste a bullet on you. 2. If the enemy is in range - SO ARE YOU. AND WHAT IS THREE?????? 3.The Sniper's motto: reach out and touch someone. Ha

CHAPTER TWELVE

ROAD TRIP TO FORT BENNING

[ROAD TRIP TO FT BENNING BEGINS]

[FADES TO BLACK]

[ON THE HIGHWAY 95 SOUTH]

[Dan and Stephanie stop for a bathroom break. Dan sees a lot of cheap fireworks for sale. While Stephanie is in the bathroom Dan runs around to purchases $300.00 worth of huge fireworks and a lot of freebees (buy 1 get 10 free). This amounts to about $2000.00 in value. Dan loads up the Vanishing Point and hides all the fireworks. He is thinking that in two months it will be New Years and he can set them off on the Beach in Ft. Lauderdale.]

[Stephanie and Dan get in the van and keep going south to get to Ft. Benning Georgia].

[As they get off the Highway they see the entrance sign for Ft. Benning but drive on to find a motel]

30 SEP 1986

1986,Fort Benning, Ranger School, Class 13

"FORT BENNING School of the Americas"

EXT. ROOM FRONT DOOR - OFF POST MOTEL FT BENNING – MORNING

[staying at the Off Post Motel just outside of Fort Benning GA. While Dan is attending his training at the School of the Americas Stephanie has to wait at the motel.
On this particular morning as Dan stepped out the front door of their motel room he noticed a suspicious car in the parking lot. Not wanting to startle Stephanie but at the same time he wants her to be aware of her surrounding and security conscious.]

DAN

Okay come give me a kiss I have to go now.

[As Dan opens the door the wind rushes in as large black car pulls into the parking lot area just outside opposite the motel room door that Dan and Stephanie are staying in]

DAN (WHISPERING)

Wait! Wait! Get back inside the room.

STEPANIE (WHISPERING)
Why! Who is out there?

DAN (WHISPERING)
I am not sure but you know we have to be more careful now.

STEPHANIE (WHISPERING)
Why?

DAN (WHISPERING)
Well I mean there are bad guys here and there. We - You need to keep an eye out for any unusual people hanging around. There is this one guy who is a real problem for people like me. [Dan peeking thru the curtain window]

STEPHANIE (WHISPERING)
Do you know his name or what he looks like?

DAN (NO LONGER WHISPERING)
I am referring to a prominent terrorist, his name is Ad. Ad Libby, "I will be glad to meet Ad Libby on equal terms anywhere in the world. I am willing to subject myself, but not you or my dad, to a fight with terrorists.

STEPHANIE (NORMAL TONE)
Really --Ad Libby? Don't you think we should get some kind motel security system? There was a commercial on TV about the "Enterprise Security System" Maybe we can find out how much it costs.

DAN (WHISPERING)
Whoever it was - they are gone now. So I am going to go. Remember what I said about keeping an eye out.

[Dan peeking thru the curtain window. Opens the door and drives away]

<u>EXT. ROAD TO FT BENNING – DAY</u>
[Dan is driving Fort Benning GA. Parks the van near the jump school and gets out with his duffle bags. Without any warning a Monty Python type short Englishman soldier with a clip board appears and begins walking with Mr. 46857 aka Dan]

SOLDIER (TRYING TO KEEP PACE)
Sir may I ask you your name?

DAN
Whose asking?

SOLDIER (TRYING TO KEEP PACE)
Well I was asked to track down this guy

(shows a photo of Dan)and you fit the description.

DAN
I would say he looks a bit like me?

SOLDIER (TRYING TO KEEP PACE)
Are you 46857?

DAN
Yes as a matter of fact some folks call me that….

SOLDIER (TRYING TO KEEP PACE)
Well sir you must follow me - straight this way.

[They walk together passing the sign - Welcome to Airborne School Ft. Benning GA. Black hats walking around yelling.]

[The Englishman soldier apparently had gotten the wrong guy. 46857 was not supposed to be at jump school. Never the less 46857 was basically grabbed and strapped into jump gear - even with his street clothes on. I remember the ungawa free tower - the black hat under me was incoherent to begin with, and imagine him talking thru a bull horn... I couldn't understand a word he said. I pissed him off real bad I guess, he PT'ed me for a good 15-20 minutes]☐

[Camera views - A quick look at one of the 34 foot towers and the 250 foot towers. The 34 foot towers simulate jumping/exiting from an Aircraft while in a parachute harness hanging from a cable, and the 250 tower gives you the opportunity to actually be under canopy, dropped after you reach the top]

DAN
Hey guys? Guys? Wait a minute!! I am not…. WAIT A MINUTE - OKAY OKAY I AM SURE ITS ALL GONNA GET BETTER IN A MINUTE!!!aaaaahhhhhh[up up and away]

[Songs fades in as Dan dangles - suspended by straps bouncing up and down at the same time in slow motion 2 other soldiers are bouncing up and down but then starts to like it…..]

[Talking Heads Music Fades in]

"Pulled Up"

Mommy, Daddy, come and look at me now
I'm a big man in a great big town
Years ago who would believe it's true
Goes to show what a little faith can do

I was complaining, I was down in the dumps
I feel so strong now 'cause you pulled me up!
Pull me up up up up up up up up

I slipped, and I got pulled
Pulled up, I tripped, and then you pulled,
you pulled me up
I slipped, and I got pulled,
Pulled up, I slipped, and then you pulled,
you pulled me up pull me up pull me up...
Pulled me up up up up up up up up

[SUBTITLES: weaponry, improvised self-defense, analytical combat, and espionage. Part of intelligence training is instruction in something called the "Dark Arts". The Dark Arts are the espionage, trickery, con artistry type stuff. Quote: It's not like being back on the block once your in - *your in.]*

[NOTE: CONTACT THE WRITER FOR RELEASABLE DECLASSIFIED STORY]

[NEXT PARAGRAPHS OF THE SCRIPT ARE OPTIONAL DEPENDING DIRECTOR'S CUT]

EXT. DAY - RANGE MASTER

[At the Firing Range - Two SME are discussing Dan's superior eyesight the level of accuracy Dan is displaying at the range. Dan's shooter skills in each weapon are at the Sharpshooter Distinguished Expert: Aggregate course of fire shot five times with a score of 201/300 or better in each aggregate - and the instructors are noticing 275 RANKS HIGH]

[Dan is entering classroom - sign on the door DESIGNATED DEFENSIVE MARKSMAN (DDM) class is in progress. Dan opens the walks in and takes a seat in a class of 20 DDM trainees]

DDM INSTRUCTOR [TO CLASS]

There are many things to know. Wind classification, wind velocity. How much effect will the wind have on the bullet? A common method of estimating velocity of the wind is to watch a flag. If no flag is visible use a piece of grass, cotton or some other light piece of material. All telescopic sights must have windage adjustments that are graduated in minutes of angle or fraction thereof. UTILIZING THE TECHNIQUES TAUGHT, ZEROING AND FIELD EXPEDIENT ZERO WILL BOOST NOT ONLY YOUR CONFIDENCE IN YOUR WEAPON BUT WILL ASSIST IN MAKING SURE YOU RETURN FROM THE MISSION - ALIVE.

[NOTE: CONTACT THE WRITER FOR CLARIFICATION ON DECLASSIFIED STORY]

[OPTIONAL DIRECTOR'S CUT]

[Fort Benning - School of the Americas SOA]

U.S. SPECIAL FORCES MAJOR "CRAFTY" SHELTON SOA INSTRUCTOR [TALKING TO NEW RECRUITS] [DEEEEP SOUTH SOUTHERN ACCENT]

I am going to show you how you can kill a man with just about anything. That is what we do in this class - we teach you how to kill, kill, KILL! You can use a bra, a pen, even a paper cup.

Friends if you never thought you couldn't kill someone… well I have got news for you!

Our country was founded on killing - just like 4th of July!

On Thanksgiving we kill a turkey

On Christmas we kill a tree

On Halloween just about everything on television is either killing or getting killed - plus we kill pumpkins cutting them up and what not.

On Easter now I still don't get it but what the hell does a rabbit have to do with eggs? Well anyway Jesus was killed and he rose from the dead - let's remember that there are popular songs - 50 ways to kill you lover, Killing Me Softly by Roberta Flack. It's A Killer by Lynyrd Skynyrd. Don't Kill It Carol by Manfred Mann's Earth Band. You Can't Kill Rock And Roll by Ozzy Osborne. Psycho Killer by The Talking Heads. She's Just Killing Me by ZZ Top. License To Kill by Bob Dylan and of course Murder She Wrote-- just to name a few…

And just so you know if Jesus Christ had taken a poll he wouldn't have gone to Jerusalem.

So whats my point? Killing is like greed and greed is good. There are two places in purgatory.

Purgatory 1: those who did it

Purgatory 2: those who did it and said they didn't do it

One of my most important pieces of advice is - EVEN A FOOT SOLDIER MUST always think out of the box. In most cases you must determine all the risk, all the possibilities when meeting assets. Also always have more than one passport stashed away including enough local currency for bribes. If you have a mission on the horizon - nobody is going to save your ass. You have to be smart enough to know the layout of the land, who your friends are, where are the safe houses, alternative navigation methods on land and at sea.

Assassin training requires discipline, loyalty, secrecy and courage. Applicants must be willing to put the CIA and the mission above all personal relationships and duties. The life of an assassin in training is very strenuous. Students are put through rigorous training exercises to cultivate discipline and a "killer instinct." Training typically lasts between six months and two years, depending on the acumen of the student and his skill level. However, training as an assassin is a lifelong process, where experience is the real teacher.

The function of a CIA assassin is to kill those who pose a threat to U.S. national security. CIA assassins have allegedly been responsible for some of the most recognized assassinations and assassination attempts in the past century. They may also be responsible for "black ops," operations that are strictly off the books--operations that governments can deny they had any involvement in. Agents killed during a black op are never recognized publicly by the government.

Remember destroy anything on you or your dead buddy that may tie you back to us. Don't leave nothing for the enemy. We don't know you and you are on your own. If your smart enough to get here then you are smart enough to get yourself out of any mess you find yourself in

Some of you guys may have ALICE - [All-purpose Lightweight Individual Carrying Equipment, an older form of combat gear still in occasional use in some Marine activities, replaced by MOLLE and ILBE]

[Dan wearing helmet and military gear high up on]

[Dan getting ready for jump week -- started jumping from 5 feet and working his way up to 1,250 no fear of heights] [Dan is one of 1,500 Soldiers attending Fort Benning's Airborne School]

[Students with A Company began the first of three phases of training, while B Company troops entered their second phase and C Company troops completed five static line jumps to earn Airborne wings.]

[During the first week, called ground week, students focus on the individual skills needed to make parachute jumps and land safely. Under the watchful eye of "Black Hats" cadre from the battalion, ground week students learn mock door exercises, conduct 34-foot tower jumps and train on the lateral drift apparatus to practice parachute landing falls.]

[Dan moved into tower week where they use the 34-foot and 250-foot towers to jump.] [Tower week builds on ground week skills and emphasizes the "mass exit" concepts the Army uses in airborne operations.]

[The students work with the 34-foot and 250-foot jump towers; swing landing trainer and suspended harness until they've mastered the landings. After two weeks of training, jump week is the test of the students' skills.]

[Students must complete five parachute jumps onto Fryar Field Drop Zone, two with combat equipment and three "Hollywood-style," only the parachute and reserve. Students who complete all five jumps earn their wings. Not every Soldier is a paratrooper. Some are scared of heights and some just aren't cut out for (Airborne School)]

[Soldiers have to be prepared for the physical aspect of it, being thrown to the ground. It takes a lot of dedication to continuously jump off a 12-foot platform and hit the ground hard]

[Completing Airborne School opens up opportunities and can help Soldiers get promoted.
This course instills students with the warrior spirit. It's not just a class, it's a way to get to work]

[B Company students will graduate Friday, followed by A Company]
[On his last jump, his main chute opened seconds before he touched the turf. The colonel directing the operation told Dan, "Sit down and rest, your color will return to your face in a few minutes]
[The black hat yells> Stand up, hook up, shuffle to the door, jump right out and count to four!]

STATIC LINE JUMPING AND HIGH ALTITUDE AND LOW OPENING (HALO) TRAINING

"Pulled Up"

Mommy, Daddy, come and look at me now
I'm a big man in a great big town
Years ago who would believe it's true
Goes to show what a little faith can do

I was complaining, I was down in the dumps
I feel so strong now 'cause you pulled me up!
Pull me up up up up up up up up

I slipped, and I got pulled
Pulled up, I tripped, and then you pulled,
you pulled me up
I slipped, and I got pulled,

Pulled up, I slipped, and then you pulled,
you pulled me up pull me up pull me up...
Pulled me up up up up up up up up

I drift away to another land
Sleeping dreaming such a simple thing

[A BIT OF HUMOR]

[MISSIONS 1,2 have talking but 3,4,5,ARE MONTAGED -

KISS STEPHANIE GOODBYE-

GO COMPLETE MISSION

HONEY I'M HOME…..][Then onto FLA for Nicawwa Mission]

CHAPTER THIRTEEN

ON A MISSION AND GETTING OUT OF TOWN

[EXT. DAY - COLUMBIA DRUG LORD'S RANCH - MISSION 1 READ KINGPIN'S LIPS AND GATHER INTEL – TAKE OUT KINGPIN - COLOMBIA]

LEAD DRUG DEALER

I know most of you guys are new to the business but whatever El Guapo ask - just say yes!

[Drug lord's gang walking into his private ranch]

EL GUAPO DRUG LORD

Welcome! Welcome to my humble abode.

(MISSION: DELTA FORCE NEEDS A LIP READER IN THE FIELD NOW. READ LIPS TO GAIN INTEL ON WHEREABOUTS KEY DRUGKINGPIN IN SA)

[Dan is dropped by helicopter in full BDU tactical camo gear. For three days he laid in wait while observing the kingpin's ranch. By the fourth day of living in the jungle he is surprised by his spotter an overweight John Candy type also donned in camo gear. The spotter almost lost his life when he surprised Dan at Dan's observation site. Dan is relooking this situation and is not sure about assassinating the kingpin after all. The spotter tells Dan the adjustment and Dan closes his eyes and shoots. Dan and the spotter makes run for it. The viewers see what really happens as Dan had shot the TV remote control on the bar. The kingpin comes in the room and blames the damaged remote on a fellow drug dealer and shots him. The bodyguard of the other deal shoots the king pin after all said and done 10 dealers and 5 body guards all shoot each other and Dan's gains notoriety as the shooter who took down the gang. News story makes the headlines and reaches the US INTEL agencies and Dan's get a pat on the back.]

MISSION TWO - CARACAS VZ

[NOTE: CONTACT DANIEL A. SHEA FOR ADDITIONAL MATERIAL ON EACH MISSION]

(MISSION ONE: DELTA FORCE NEEDS A LIP READER IN THE FIELD NOW. THEY HAVE A HIGH VALUE TARGET [HVT] UNDER SURVIELLANCE AND NEED INTEL ANY WAY THAT IT CAN BE OBTAINED. DF COMMANDER REQUEST TO PULL DAN FROM TRAINING AND DEPOLY TO FIELD [VENEZUELA] TO BE A PART OF A 3 MEMBER SURVIELLANCE TEAM. CASTRO'S DOCTOR IB)

SURVIELLANCE TEAM LEAD
Greetings Mr. 46857. Heard a lot of things about you.

DAN (AS 46857 TEMPORARY NOM DE GUERRE)
Good to meet you am I killing anyone today?

SURVIELLANCE CARACAS TEAM LEAD
No no this is a surveillance operation. We are watching a VIP. This is a targeting opportunity since our mark, our target is staying here where we can observe her.

DAN (AS 46857)

Could I ask for more information? The type of case it is?

SURVIELLANCE CARACAS TEAM LEAD
No you cannot. This is a very sensitive case. I can however tell you since you are here to read her lips - she is Castro's doctor. Well one of his special doctors. Her name is Iraida Briceno de Espino. She is a skin doctor of some kind. Find out what she is saying, translate it for us and we will see if she is a good candidate to come work for us.

DAN (AS 46857)
Really we are going to recruit her?

SURVIELLANCE CARACAS TEAM LEAD

Depends on what you tell us. She might be key in getting into Castro's inner circle. Shit! Now you made me talk to much dammit! Get you head gear on and mike - get moving time is passing.

[For three days Dan watches and translates the Dra Briceno's conversation thru his binoculars. Thinking out of the box he attempts to get closer to the mark to really get a feel about her personality]

[Gear used to perform missions][FORT BENNING ROADTRIP ENDS][FADE TO BLACK]

CHAPTER FOURTEEN

MIAMI ROAD TRIP

[Shea Graduated FT Benning SOA – On the way to MIAMI For Mission 3 – ROAD TRIP 95 SOUTH: Head to Florida]

[Dan and Stephanie (per Nicky's orders in double wrapped brown envelop). Arrive in Miami and check into the Club Caribbean Motel on U.S. 1. During check in there is the most annoying agent working the front desk. After a long drive Dan has no patience during check in. Each time the desk agent said "ummm, ummm, ummm" Dan was reaching for his 45 cal tuck in belt on his back side. From the rear view Dan would reach for it and Stephanie would put her hand on his hand over the 45 so he wouldn't pull it out. Dan was having flash backs to the Nun in elementary school as she too would also say "ummmm, ummm, ummmmm"!]

DESK AGENT (TO DAN AND STEPHANIE)

oh that wasn't so bad was it. I am getting better at checking in folks

STEPHANIE

Well yes and no – but hey you are not blonde for nothing

DESK AGENT (TO DAN AND STEPHANIE)

Yes I am not blonde for nothing hmmmm not blonde for nothing. (pondering if that is good or bad)

NICKY (PHONE CALL TO DAN)

Hello Dan. How did it go in training?

DAN

Hey NicK this is a nice surprise. It went well. Lots of interesting folks back there.

NICKY (PHONE CALL TO DAN)

Dan I am in Miami and I want to meet with you at Miami International Airport a place known as "Corrosion Corner" it has all the aging airplanes parked in a sprawling system of aviation lots. Can you find it? Remind me that I have a job for you in Miami before you go downrange.

DAN
Sure no problem.

NICKY (PHONE CALL TO DAN)
Meet me there and I take you over to introduce you to Southern Air Transport management. Corporate AIR and then the UNO Miami headquarters just across NW 36th Street from Southern Air.

(EXT. MIAMI AIRPORT - SIGNS IN BACKGROUND - CORPORATE AIR, SOUTHERN AIR TRANSPORT.)

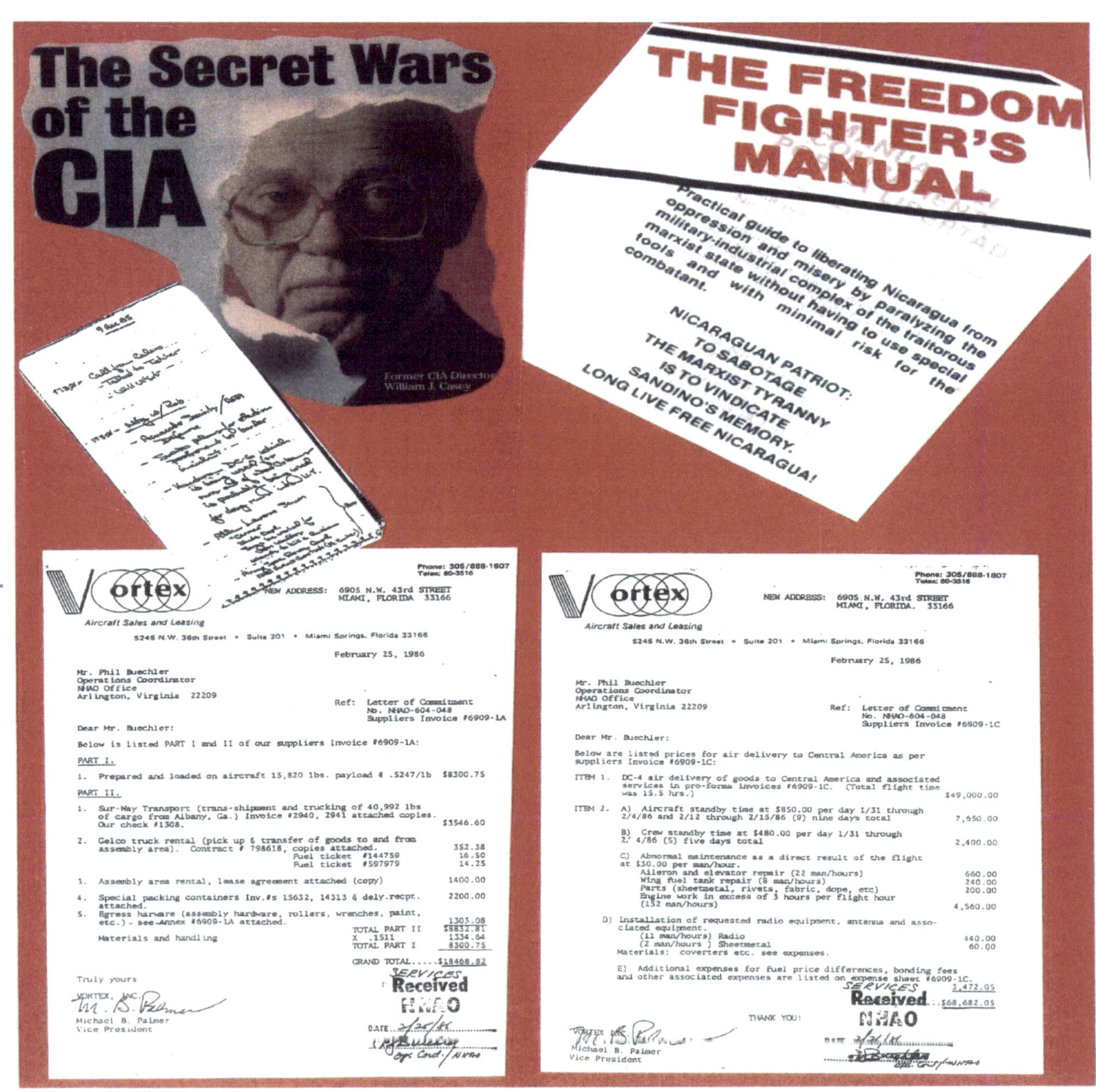

Vortex
Aircraft Sales and Leasing
5245 N.W. 36th Street • Suite 201 • Miami Springs, Florida 33166
Phone: 305/888-1807
Telex: 80-3516
NEW ADDRESS: 6905 N.W. 43rd STREET MIAMI, FLORIDA 33166

February 25, 1986

Mr. Phil Buechler
Operations Coordinator
NHAO Office
Arlington, Virginia 22209

Ref: Letter of Commitment No. NHAO-604-048 Suppliers Invoice #6909-1A

Dear Mr. Buechler:

Below is listed PART I and II of our suppliers Invoice #6909-1A:

PART I.

1. Prepared and loaded on aircraft 15,820 lbs. payload @ .5247/1b $8300.75

PART II.

1. Sur-Way Transport (trans-shipment and trucking of 40,992 lbs of cargo from Albany, Ga.) Invoice #2940, 2941 attached copies. Our check #1308. $3546.60
2. Gelco truck rental (pick up & transfer of goods to and from assembly area). Contract # 798618, copies attached. 352.38
   Fuel ticket #144759 16.50
   Fuel ticket #597979 14.25
3. Assembly area rental, lease agreement attached (copy) 1400.00
4. Special packing containers Inv.#s 15632, 14313 & dely.recpt. attached. 2200.00
5. Egress harware (assembly hardware, rollers, wrenches, paint, etc.) - see Annex #6909-1A attached. 1303.08

TOTAL PART II $8832.81
Materials and handling X .1511 1334.64
TOTAL PART I 8300.75

GRAND TOTAL.....$18468.82

Truly yours
VORTEX, INC.
Michael B. Palmer
Vice President

SERVICES Received NHAO
DATE 2/26/86
Ops. Coord./NHAO

Vortex
Aircraft Sales and Leasing
5245 N.W. 36th Street • Suite 201 • Miami Springs, Florida 33166
Phone: 305/888-1807
Telex: 80-3516
NEW ADDRESS: 6905 N.W. 43rd STREET MIAMI, FLORIDA. 33166

February 25, 1986

Mr. Phil Buechler
Operations Coordinator
NHAO Office
Arlington, Virginia 22209

Ref: Letter of Commitment No. NHAO-604-048 Suppliers Invoice #6909-1C

Dear Mr. Buechler:

Below are listed prices for air delivery to Central America as per suppliers Invoice #6909-1C:

ITEM 1. DC-4 air delivery of goods to Central America and associated services in pro-forma invoices #6909-1C. (Total flight time was 15.5 hrs.) $49,000.00

ITEM 2. A) Aircraft standby time at $850.00 per day 1/31 through 2/4/86 and 2/12 through 2/15/86 (9) nine days total 7,650.00

B) Crew standby time at $480.00 per day 1/31 through 2/4/86 (5) five days total 2,400.00

C) Abnormal maintenance as a direct result of the flight at $30.00 per man/hour.
Aileron and elevator repair (22 man/hours) 660.00
Wing fuel tank repair (8 man/hours) 240.00
Parts (sheetmetal, rivets, fabric, dope, etc) 200.00
Engine work in excess of 3 hours per flight hour (152 man/hours) 4,560.00

D) Installation of requested radio equipment, antenna and associated equipment.
(11 man/hours) Radio 440.00
(2 man/hours) Sheetmetal 60.00
Materials: coverters etc. see expenses.

E) Additional expenses for fuel price differences, bonding fees and other associated expenses are listed on expense sheet #6909-1C. 3,472.05

$68,682.05

THANK YOU!

VORTEX INC.
Michael B. Palmer
Vice President

SERVICES Received NHAO
DATE 2/26/86
Ops. Coord./NHAO

Shooters
VALET
PARKING

NICKY (MEETING DAN)
Hey man good to see you after all this time. Are you doing ok?

DAN
Yes man doing well,doing well.

NICKY (MEETING DAN)
Are you still with - whatz her name Stephanie Loose Mantle piece or are you single?

DAN
Yes I am still with Stephanie - you know the co-habitation test.

NICKY
Yep that's it - Stephanie! The name slipped my mind for a minute. You didn't bring her here did you?

DAN
. No no - not to the airport. (under his breath) But yes to Miami.

NICKY
Oh wow man you are crazy! She could jeopardize your whole operation! That girl is like fire and ice. I have some advice - send her back! Back! Back now! How is the co-habitation going?

DAN
No no I am not going to do that….. shes changed. Changed a little bit BUT she is a sloppy slob

NICKY
Oh yeah how? How did she changed? Oh wow man you are crazy!

DAN
Well she has gotten better that she doesn't talk over me that much. She does leave the toilet seat up and she does do a good massage. No no I am not going to send her back up north. It will be ok.

NICKY
Ok but I am warning you. This operation is top shelf stuff you got it? If she interferes in any way I am going to have my guys take her to Niagara Falls. Do you read me?

DAN
Okay understood.

NICKY

Grab that backpack and the clip board. These are the items I need you to pick up for the downrange folks. This fedex envelop has cash in it $16,000.00. You don't need to send but hold on to it because a lady is coming in from Washington DC. Her name is Shirley. You will need to give her the cash and she will give you two KL-43s. Do you know what KL-43s are?

DAN

Yes I do. I had the training when I was at THE FARM.

DAN

[Reading from the list] Three uzis, 20 45ACPs, 30 silencers oh sure no problem. I can take care of this.

[High fiving] [Walking away]

NICKY (MEETING DAN)

Ok good - and don't forget ship that Greek bitty back north!! It will add a few years to your life!

(EXT. MIAMI - SIGNS IN BACKGROUND - CORPORATE AIR, SOUTHERN AIR TRANSPORT, UNO HEADQUARTERS (THESE SIGNS ARE MEANT TO BE COMICAL AS THEY ARE REAL NAMES OF THE ENTERPRISE)

(EXT. MIAMI - VANINSHING POINT)

[Dan has been driving all over Miami collecting equipment on the list that Nicky gave him. However, the van is loaded with guns, weapons, knifes and cammo gear for downrange folks.
(After Dan picks up Stephanie she notices there are a lot of items in the van. Dan just realizes that he has to get to a meeting to drop off the supplies so that they make the next flight. Driving fast -- Dan has to step on the brakes rather hard to avoid running a red light. Just then the guns MAC10 come sliding out from under the passenger seat - STEPHANIE FREAKS OUT!!!)

[BREAKS COME TO SCREECHING HALT……….]

STEPHANIE (TO DAN)

WHAT THE HELL! WHAT THE HELL IS THIS???? Wait wait wait - stop the CAR!!! STOP THE CAR NOW!!!

DAN

WAIT! WAIT! Wait I can explain. I can explain can you please calm down. I can explain but right now I have to drop this stuff off.

[Dan is driving down alley ways between EMPTY WHAREHOUSE buildings trying to make his meeting]

[Stephanie reaches over and grabs the steering wheel forcing Dan to almost crash but comes to a complete screeching halt].

[Stephanie whips open the passenger door, grabs a back pack of MAC10s, 45APCs and one modified combat shotgun. She jumps out with the bag and one gun in her hand.]

[Dan whips open the driver side door, grabs a back pack of MAC10s, and 45APCs]

STEPHANIE (ACTING LIKE SHE IS IN THE MOVIES)
WHOSE BAD NOW SUCKA!!!!!

[Stephanie aiming the gun at Dan's feet and start shooting bam! Bam! Bam!]

DAN
[Running] WAIT! WAIT! Wait I can explain. I can explain can you please calm down. STOP! STOP! Don't shoot I don't know if its loaded! Guns are dangerous. You should never point a gun at someone unless you intend to use it. I am warning you - knock it OFFFFFFF!!!!!

[Dan cocks his MAC10 and shoots near Stephanie's feet BAM!, BAM, BAM, BAM!!]

[Instead of Stephanie getting scared she gets more angry and has two MAC 10s one in each hand and starts firing toward Dan's feet] BAM! BAM! BAM! Wow cool ha ha!

[Both are firing at the same time]

[Dan shooting at the ground near Stephanie]

STEPHANIE
GOT YOU NOW SUCKA!!!!! [LAUGHING OUT LOUD]

DAN
[Yelling over the gun shooting] WILL YOU STOP IT! THIS IS NOT A FRICKIN MOVIE!! Come on seriously. I am working on a government project and I need to drop this cargo before they depart. Will just get back in the van?

[both are out of bullets guns smoking]

STEPHANIE
OK BUSTER BUT YOU BETTER TELL ME EVERYTHING!!!!! [LAUGHING OUT LOUD] [Getting back in the van] That was cool. I have never fired a gun before. Kiss me, kiss me KISS ME!! Oooohh you make me soooo HOT!

[Stephanie is pulling Dan from the driver's side to the middle of the van trying to kiss him after nearly killing him]

DAN
[Starting the van] Did you ever hear of

Bay of Pigs?

STEPHANIE

Bay of Pigs? No I don't like to eat pork.

DAN

The Bay of Pigs was a historical event around the time of when President Kennedy "JFK" was in office.

STEPHANIE

I WAS TO YOUNG TO CARE

[From the passenger seat looking in the back in the van]   That was really cool. What else do you have back there?

[Stephanie unzips the nearest backpack and discovers bricks of $100.00 bills (millions)]

Beautiful exchange rate $300.00 to $1.00 American Dollar.

STEPHANIE

No way…….

DAN

Way……….

[Stephanie and Dan arrive at the meeting place (back alley behind warehouse) and no one is there. They are late and missed the rendezvous]

DAN

[Shaking his head] You see Stephanie! Do you see what you've done? My contacts are already gone. They have no idea what has happened. They might think that I have drove off with the money and guns.

Now I have to drive around with all this money and guns for a few days until the next plane is ready!

(INT. MIAMI - DAY - CLUB CARIBBEAN MOTEL 5:00AM)

[Dan sleeping and rolls over on top of Stephanie while she is sleeping. He begins kissing her and she is kissing him and he is completely out of it [asleep]. In the middle of kissing he awakes and says--

DAN

[Realizing that he is kissing in his sleep]Oh oh OMG I am sorry I thought you were someone else......

STEPHANIE

[whispering in Dan's ear] Dan I am sorry. I am sorry you missed your meeting yesterday. Are you like on a secret mission or something? Okay then do you like my beautiful brown bedroom eyes? [smiling]

DAN [NOT SAYING ANYTHING]

STEPHANIE

Oooooh that's a yes. Okay okay I want to be Vanna Vanna White, No Stella White!

DAN

Vanna White? Are you kidding me she is a television personality? You would want to keep a low profile.

STEPHANIE

Okay how about Fawn like a little baby deer with brown eyes? I like that Fawn. Fawn Hall with beautiful brown bedroom eyes. Or STELLA!! Yes I will be Stella and what is your name do you need one? Have one? Waiting on one? Come on tell me. I can help you. I can type I'll have you know.

DAN

[pulling to blankets over his head] Stephanie I am sleeping. Will you leave me alone.

STEPHANIE

[Looking in the mirror at herself] Ooooh I am so excited! Dan do you like my brown eyes? Dan? Dan do you like my beautiful brown bedroom eyes? Come on wake up talk to me!

DAN

[under the blanket] Do you know how to spell codependent?

STEPHANIE

Wake up! Let's go to the Fort Lauderdale boardwalk

and see the nightclubs.
[looking in Dan's bag] Can I use these travelers checks I just need $60.00 to take to the beach.

DAN

Okay okay I'm up. Let's go.

EXT. FORT LAUDERDALE BOARDWALK - EVENING - SUN IS SETTING

Penrod's
SEASONS GREETINGS
FROM THE
PENRODS GANG

[STEPHANIE AND DAN AT PENRODS]

UNITED STATES OF AMERICA
INTERNATIONAL MOTOR TRAFFIC

ernational Driving Per
vention on International Road Traffic of 19 September 1949
(United Nations)

ed at FALLS CHURCH, VIRGINIA 22047, U.S.A.
Valid For One Year From:
28 December 1983

IMPORTANT — This permit is not valid for driving in the United States

THE AMERICAN AUTOMOBILE ASSOCIATION INCORPORATED AAA CONNECTICUT-1910

J. B. Creal
Authorized signature of the empowered authority

Nº 902597

[WET T-SHIRT CONTEST]

[Dan and Stephanie wander around Pen Rods on the Fort Lauderdale strip. Just checking out the skyline, beach, all the action. Eventually they come across a club for wet t-shirt contest. Stephanie is trying to be nice to Dan and thinks he'll have fun going to see a wet t-shirt contest. WRONG! Dan doesn't want to be in large crowds, drinking and yelling. But after going inside at Stephanie's behest he starts to get into it and doesn't want to leave.]

STEPHANIE

Dan check this out - should be fun.

DAN

No not really its too many people inside and the line is too long. Lets go somewhere else. I was hoping for something more quieter

STEPHANIE

Please, please, pretty please! I have to go pee….

DAN

Okay fine you go in and meet me at the bar. I will come in and in front of everyone I will try to pick you up.

STEPH

Okay fine- like role playing?

DAN
Exactly!!

[Dan and Steph wait in line but then Stephanie runs past the bouncer. Dan tries to follow her and gets stopped by a 250 pound ten foot tall red neck bouncer]

[Steph heads to the ladies room]

BOUNCER TO DAN
Hey whoa! whoa boy! Wherd did ya'll think ya going?

BARTENDER
Welcome to Club X my name is Brendan what can I get for you and do you have any questions.

DAN
Yes hello. I would like coke, a menu, and how much for the whore at the end of the bar?

[Bartender unaware Dan and Steph are together. He tries to scam Dan. The bartender sees Stephanie waiting to use the ladies room and he is trying to come up with a price as he is checking out her looks]

BARTENDER
Hmmm the whore. The whore is going for $350.00 an hour.

DAN
$350 an hour why that's highway robbery! I mean look at her big fat ass, scrungy hair, pathetic hips, I mean she can't be worth more than a mere fifty bucks and not a dime more!

BARTENDER (LYING)
Well there is a referral fee. So its $350 dollars.

[Meanwhile the ugliest girl in the joint comes over and sits in the chair next to Dan]

DAN
[staring at the ugly girl] Pardon me are you gonna sit there all night?

UGLY GIRL
Yeah why whatz it to you!

DAN
Aww just my luck!!

Hey ugly if you were a guy and I not saying you are -- how much would you pay for the whore at the end of the bar?

UGLY GIRL
pfffft! [rolls her eyes]
$100 bucks!

[Stephanie is suspicious about their conversation]

[Dan proceeds over to where Stephanie is sitting. He turns his back to her and begins chatting with a beautiful buxomly blonde. Steph motions her hands up in the air mouthing "WTF" - after a few minutes she doesn't care about role playing and is getting pissed at Dan for ignoring her. The blonde is getting pissed at Steph - can only mean one thing - CAT FIGHT!!]

STEPHANIE
Dan lets go dance!

BLONDE
HEY!! LET GO I FOUND HIM FIRST!! [SHOVING

STEPH BACK]

[After a wrestle between Steph and Blonde - Steph wins]

DAN
Aww just my luck!! I don't wanna dance.

STEPHANIE
It'll be fun.

[Stephanie takes a reluctant Dan up to the dance floor. Dan's lightbulb goes on (idea). He will dance so bad to embarrass Stephanie] Dan starts dancing like a dork.] [Audience is watching and bar tender keeps making finger movements as in where is my money for the whore]

[Song kicks in]

"Shut Up And Dance"

"Oh don't you dare look back.
Just keep your eyes on me."
I said, "You're holding back, "
She said, "Shut up and dance with me!"
This woman is my destiny
She said, "Ooh-ooh-hoo,
Shut up and dance with me."

"Don't you dare look back.
Just keep your eyes on me."
I said, "You're holding back, "
She said, "Shut up and dance with me!"
This woman is my destiny
She said, "Ooh-ooh-hoo,
Shut up and dance with me."

[AFTER LEAVING THE CLUB DAN & STEPHANIE ARE WALKING ON THE BEACH. DAN TELLS STEPHANIE WAIT BY THE STAIRS NEAR THE SIDEWALK.] [HE TELLS STEPHANIE HE HAS A SURPRISE AND HE'LL BE RIGHT BACK. DAN HURRIES OFF TO THE VANISHING POINT AND UNLOADS ALL THE FIREWORKS HE BOUGHT IN SOUTH CAROLINA. JUST DOWN A BIT FROM WHERE STEPHANIE IS HE WIRES TOGETHER ALL THE LARGE FIREWORKS TO GO OFF AT THE SAME TIME. AFTER HE FINISHED HE RAN DOWN THE BEACH TO GET STEPH. WHEN THEY RETURN DAN HAS A LIGHTER IN HIS HAND GETTING READY TO LIGHT WHEN THE CLOCK TICKS MIDNIGHT - JUST THEN 5 POLICE OFFICERS DRIVING ATV OFFROAD VEHICLES SHOW UP. THEY ARE LAUGHING SO HARD AS THEY HAVE NEVER SEEN SO MUCH FIREWORKS. THEY ASK DAN IF IT HIS AND HE SAYS NO. DAN ASKED IF IT WAS ILLEGAL AND THE OFFICER SAYS - INTERSTATE TRANSPORTATION OF EXPLOSIVES. DAN AND STEPH BEGIN TO WALK AWAY [DAN IS IN THE MIDDLE OF SAYING"ITS ALL GONNA GET BETTER IN A MINUTE"…. STEPHANIE GRABS THE LIGHTER - ON HER HANDS AND KNEES SNEAKS UP BEHIND THE OFFICERS AND AT THE STROKE OF MIDNIGHT SHE LIGHTS THE FIREWORKS - IT ALL BLAST OFF - THE POLICE RUN AWAY—DAN AND STEPHANIE RUNS AWAY….. DAN YELLS AT HER "ARE YOU CARZY"?

[NEXT DAY EXT HOTEL PARKING LOT. DAN IS LOADING SUITCASE AND TAKING STEPHANIE TO THE AIRPORT.FROM A DISTANCE YOU SEE STEPHANIE WAVING HER ARMS PACING BACK AND FORTH ADAMANT SHE IS NOT GOING TO THE AIRPORT. WHEN THEY ARRIVE AT THE AIRPORT SHE IS ADAMANT THAT SHE IS NOT GETTING OUT OF THE CAR.DAN CARRIES STEPHANIE OVER HIS SHOULDER FROM THE CAR TO THE PLANE TO SEND HER BACK TO BOSTON.]

Having fun at Club Caribbean in Florida with my Marine buddy and his girlfriend after Stephanie left.

[AS STEPHANI IS FLYING AWAY ON THE PLANE MUSIC FADES IN AS SHE VISUALIZES DAN'S FACE AND THE GOOD TIMES]

"Once In A Lifetime"

And you may find yourself living in a
shotgun shack
And you may find yourself in another part
of the world
And you may find yourself behind the
wheel of a large automobile
And you may find yourself in a beautiful
house, with a beautiful
wife
And you may ask yourself-Well...How did I
get here?

money's gone
Once in a lifetime/water flowing
underground.

And you may ask yourself
What is that beautiful house?

And you may ask yourself
Where does that highway go?
And you may ask yourself
Am I right?...Am I wrong?
And you may tell yourself
MY GOD!...WHAT HAVE I DONE?

Same as it ever was...Same as it ever was...Same as it ever was...
Same as it ever was...Same as it ever was...Same as it ever was...
Same as it ever was...Same as it ever was...

STEPHANIE (TALKING OUTLOUD TO HERSELF)

[BACK IN BOSTON: Stephanie watching the TV news as a breaking news report comes on about the plane shot down in Nicaragua]

[ON TV]TV NEWS REPORTER

[ON TV]TOPICS IN THE NEWS

Russia
Following a number of trouble free years in Space Exploration the Space Shuttle Challenger explodes shortly after takeoff watched by people live on TV around the world. Back to this story in a moment.

On October 5, 1986 Nicaragua shot down a SAT C-123K, Corporate Air Services HPF821,[5] formerly USAF 54-679 (c/n 20128), cargo plane with a Soviet-supplied, shoulder-launched heat-seeking missile and captured the cargo handler, a SAT employee Eugene Hasenfus, exposing the Iran-Contra affair.

Early this morning an American C-123 was shot down over Nicaragua, three individuals on board -- the pilot, William "Bill" Cooper, co-pilot Wallace "Buzz" Sawyer,and a Nicaraguan crew member -- were killed in the crash. One man, a "kicker" by the name of Eugene Hasenfus, survived.

STEPHANIE (TALKING OUTLOUD TO HERSELF)

Oh my God!! That was Dan's mission 3. Dan said he was going to Nicarawawa!!!!! [mispronounced on purpose]

Before

Iran – Contra

North came into the public spotlight as a result of the Iran-Contra affair, a political scandal of the late 1980s, in which he claimed partial responsibility for the sale of weapons via intermediaries to Iran, with the profits being channeled to the Contras in Nicaragua. He was reportedly responsible for the establishment of a covert network, which aided the Contras.

THE NEW REPUBLIC
CASEY'S C.I.A.
Is there intelligence at the top?
by Morton Kondracke

BG
March 17, 1986
Page 3

IVAN RIVERA (DAVID)
Miami 305-554-5947 (friend)
305-594-3783 (work)

the following names have been used in connection with Seacords operation:

- Tom Clines
- Larry Sterns
- George Stockman
- Patrice Gentry
- Peter (aka Pablo) Duncan
- Alberto Coppo (in Peru)
- Antonio Molina (Hondo Colonel)
- One Lt. Col. Oliver North
- Star Production
- General Equipment and Leasing Corp. in Geneva
- Stanford Technologies Trading Group and Transfer Ltd. in Arlington,Va.

703-524-2053

305 387-2594 (H)
Martin 305 673-9506

The word is these people and companies have been involved in the procurement and transportation of arms and aircraft for the FDN. Some people are complaining these people are making money on sweetheart deals and that the prices they are getting are not as good as they could be.

On several occasions Adolfo even complained to me about Seacords and the deal he has got. Because Seacords is connected to Gadd, Adolfo has told people he had no choice but to use him.

Among the people talking openly about these deals are:

- Carl Jenkins
- Col. Bob K. Brown
- Ed Dearborn
- Individuals in Guatemala
- Individuals in Miami

In all probability, they are talking and bad mouthing Seacords because they want part of the action. They are also blaming Seacords for whatever problem arises.

As an added problem, Mario told me in Miami why Adolfo and company are upset with me and freezing me out. I am looked on as the responsible party for a number of the problems they are having. They look at me as the one carrying the water for you. They are also saying I am intimately tied to Seacords. Among things they connect me to are:

- The purchase of the Mahls at a higher price than necessary
- Stopping the export of the Lady Ellen helicopter
- Bringing Gadd into the picture, which they are not happy with
- Stopping NHAO from funding the movement of the Push and Pull and the heliocourier, which were donated and are in Hawaii
- The use of Project Hope
- Being the Godfather and promoter of Carlos Ulvert
- Thus being responsible for the move against Bosco

Adolfo [illegible] may even have thought Seacords was the one behind his not being able to buy from the Supermarket in Honduras.

Granted, alot of this may be speculation on Mario's part and others, but the perception is there. They want me out of the way; they do not trust me; and I do not believe they trust you anymore. There is still a belief the FDN can do it ~~alone and does not need~~ any help.

North
November 26, 1985
Page 3

to make contact with the different Indian and Creole factions below Bluefields. He will make a survey, find the needs, leave some radio communications equipment and set up some signals for drops. Upon returning to Costa Rica he will help establish a staff and support structure. He has met with Carlos Ulvert and JenneLee and is accepted by both.

The main problem with the South is there is no structure for Kisan and there are some elected Kisan members who will not accept Jennelee. By rights she should be the political leader down there. We are trying to make it look like all supplies come through her. The problem is Wycliff Diego does not want to fully support her.

The best bet is to develop a structure for her. A military leader must be found to take that weight off her.

Unfortunately another crazy gringo is running around in Costa Rica saying he personnally represents the State Department and the White House. He goes by John Kattle, but that is not his real name. He has talked to Cruz and others and those we do not have contact with are believing him. Joe is working on trying to get him cut off.

III. One of Brooklyn's boys called me collect yesterday and said he wants to meet me next time I go down there.

IV. Costa Rican Situation

Under Carlos Ulvert, great strides have been made. Blackie is looking for a military coordinator who has the background necessary to accomplish something positive. With Carlos' help it may be possible.

A major problem is the inability to bring in goods from the outside. These goods would include boots, pacs, uniforms. To accomplish I would suggest a meeting between you and Pizza. If he is going along with the other project, I'd think he would allow humanitariun goods to be brought in the country. Also, it would not be a bad idea for you to stroke him a little more. This last bit is from Joe.

Should it be needed, we have been offered a 74 ft. fishing boat which can carry more than 50,000 lbs. It has radar which reaches out 80 miles as well as the latest navigation equipment. The owner will allow it to be used for whatever purposes necessary. It is located in Punteranous and in great shape. Could be used to bring things down from Salvador.

If a liaison is needed to work with the field I and Joe would suggest using Felipe Vidal. A Cuban who knows the area, knows the groups and the terrain.

V. Project Hope

Spent over an hour on the phone with Dr. Walsh tonight (Wednesday). He was beside himself. Duemling okayed the Grant for $6.9 million for medical goods this afternoon, then an hour later one of his people call John and told him they got to change the Grant and want to lower the amount. Walsh was furious and wants to know what is going on. To add to that Calero wants to cut the Grant, yet Duemling has already committed to Dr. Walsh the $6.9 million. Hopefully it will be worked out to Dr. Walsh's satisfaction.

HAPPY THANKSGIVING

Duemling: 6.9 mil/1104

TO: Steel Hammer, Spark Plug

March 26, 1985

FROM: TC

SUBJECT: Visit South

- The package was delivered. Some concern on Junior's part that it would not be enough, but the next day he said there would be no problem.

  I learned that the party in question was about to be denounced by his people for negotiating with the Sandinistas. They did say they would wait until he returned. If he came back firm in his stance, there would be no problem, otherwise they will go public and say he no longer represents them.

  Both Indian groups are now discussing the possibility of a merger.

- Two problems plague the Southern Front: Lack of Nicaraguan Leadership and Lack of Resourses.

  Leadership: I attended a meeting between John, Lacayo, Jesus, Mindietta, and the older Pastora. John was told by Lacayo that he was over all responsible for the southern organization in that zone, while Jesus was suppose to be the military person.

  Unfortunately a problem has arisen in the form of a Cuban who goes by Rene. He has authorized and supervised two plane loads of material coming in from Salvador. No one new about either one, nor about where the material is or what it consisted of. The only reason we found out about either one was because of happenstance.

  Until this problem is resolved a hold should be put on any material leaving Salvador for the South.

  A strong capable Nicaraguan leader must be found for the South.

- Pastora has told his people new arms will start flowing into the South within the next 15 days.

  In the past several weeks several DC-3 loads of equipment have been flow into Costa Rica by Pastora's people.

At the apex of the scandal, Lieut. Colonel North is sworn in at the Iran-*contra* hearings

Finally unshackled by the special prosecutor, unburdened of bitterness, the central figure in the Iran–contra scandal returns as

The Unsinkable Ollie North

By BARRETT SEAMAN

The tradecraft was vintage North. Once a week, usually a Monday, from June 1990 to last August, writer William Novak would fly from Boston to Washington's Dulles International, where he would take a ground-floor room at the airport Marriott Hotel. North, traveling as "Mr. Smith," would arrive separately by car, park out back and slip into Novak's room through the back door. Using a Toshiba laptop computer, the pair would then work through the day and into the evening on a document that would remain secret until barely a week before it was published. When room service delivered their evening meals, North, ever clandestine, would hide in the bathroom.

The idea of keeping the Smith Project top secret was shared by the New York publisher HarperCollins, largely for the promotional value; by North's lawyers, who were concerned that research for the book might be subpoenaed by prosecutors; and by North himself, who remains incorrigibly, unabashedly enamored of cloak-and-dagger operations. The notorious Colonel North, known by a variety of code names and aliases since his days in Vietnam (Blue, Steelhammer and Mr. Goode, among them), would later laugh that his publisher "did a helluva lot better at keeping secrets than the U.S. government."

The time for keeping secrets will never completely pass for Oliver North. He was careful to have his book vetted by the appropriate federal agencies and did not object to the few exclusions sought by the Pentagon, CIA and NSC, most of them potential clues to the identity of intelligence sources and methods. But the time for blind loyalty is past.

In *Under Fire,* North certainly fires back at those who turned on him during the Iran-*contra* battle. His disdain for Congress, the press and the special prosecutor's office is almost palpable. He ends his thank-yous to those who helped him produce the book with this curt reference to the special prosecutor: "Larry Walsh was no help at all." George Shultz is blistered for what North sees as a calculated distancing of himself from policies only after their failure was assured. His disillusionment with many he had thought to be comrades in the global war against terrorism and communism is detailed. He pieces together the disparate shards of evidence that accumulated over the five years since the scandal broke into a compelling mosaic that declares, in effect, "Yes, you dummy, of course Ronald Reagan knew what was going on! How could he not?"

There are those who will say North has been cunningly selective in his reconstruction. Bill Casey, dead and gone, will never be able to refute North's detailed account of his management of Iran-*contra's* complexities, while sitting officials like George Bush and Robert Gates get what amounts to a free pass. North would challenge that. While

Nov. 25, 1986: Reagan and Meese disclose the Iran-*contra* "diversion" and North's dismissal

sive responsibility of one mid-level staff assistant at the National Security Council (and perhaps his immediate superior, the National Security Adviser), and that this staffer had acted on his own (however unlikely that might be), and that, now that you mention it, his activities might even be criminal—if the public and the press focused on that, then maybe you didn't have another Watergate on your hands after all. Especially if you insisted that the President knew nothing about it.

I had expected to leave, and maybe even be fired—but not quite so publicly. Still, I'd had plenty of warning that my days at the NSC were numbered. I was, after all, deeply involved in two major, secret and politically explosive projects, the Iran initiative and the *contras*, and both had begun to unravel a few weeks earlier.

Shortly after the Sandinistas shot down a *contra* resupply plane with American Eugene Hasenfus on board, William Casey, the director of the CIA, had said of the operation, "Shut it down and clean it up." Somebody's head would have to roll, and offering me up as a political

I thought so too.

And now, five years later, I am even more convinced: *President Reagan knew everything.*

Ronald Reagan knew of and approved a great deal of what went on with both the Iranian initiative and private efforts on behalf of the *contras*, and he received regular, detailed briefings on both. He met on several occasions with private donors to the resistance and, it appears, personally asked a foreign leader—King Fahd of Saudi Arabia—to double his contribution. I have no doubt that he was told about the use of residuals for the *contras*, and that he approved it. Enthusiastically.

There is an additional possibility: people around the President, and perhaps even President Reagan himself, were involved in an effort to protect the highest office in the land—and the man who occupied it.

In his memoirs, Ronald Reagan wrote, "We sent word to the lawyers representing Oliver North and John Poindexter, who knew what had happened, that I wanted them to tell the entire truth and do nothing to protect

GRAN MARCHA
NACIONAL
CAMPESINA
ZUMPANGO Y
TEOLOYUCAN
FIRMES ANTE LO
C.C.C.!
CENTRAL CAMPESINA
CARDENISTA
004007

Beirut editor who disclosed Iran deal is shot

Associated Press

BEIRUT – The Lebanese journalist who disclosed the secret US arms sales to Iran was shot and wounded yesterday by a gunman riding a motorcycle.

A doctor said Hassan Sabra, publisher and editor of the Beirut weekly magazine Ash-Shiraa, may have been blinded by the gunfire. Sabra, 38, suffered four bullet wounds in the head, neck and chest from the assassination attempt.

"He is in stable condition but might lose his eyesight from the head wound," said a doctor at the American University Hospital as Sabra emerged from three hours of surgery to remove the bullets.

Sabra, a Shiite Moslem, made enemies through his reporting in Ash-Shiraa on Iranian politics and the foreign hostages held in Lebanon.

He was heading to the magazine's office in Moslem West Beirut in a chauffeur-driven car when the assailant opened fire.

Police said Sabra was in the back seat with his 12-year-old daughter, Nissrin, who suffered a minor injury from a bullet that grazed the left side of her chest.

Sabra's driver, who doubles as a bodyguard, told reporters he jumped out of the car and fired his pistol at the fleeing assailants on the motorcycle. "But I do not know whether the assailant was hit," the driver said.

Police said the body of an unidentified man bearing bullet wounds was taken to the American University Hospital two hours after the attack on Sabra.

News clipping of Editor who broke the news about Iran-Contra.

CHAPTER FIFTEEN

DOWN RANGE

(NEWS FLASH PHOTO MONTAGE: Hasenfus was captured on Oct. 6, a day after parachuting from a C-123 transport plane shot down by Nicaraguan soldiers over southern Nicaragua. On Monday, the Sandinista Justice Ministry formally charged him with trying to overthrow the Nicaraguan government, along with joining criminal groups and participating in an act of terrorism.)

HONDURAS
1987
Main Contra base camp
Miskito Indians
EL SALVADOR
=Government Control: Sandinista Front of National Liberation (FSLN)
Leon
Corinto
NICARAGUA
Managua
Grenada
Bluefields
=Guerrilla Activity: Nicaraguan Democratic Front (FDN) ("Contras")
© 2000 Matthew White
COSTA RICA

EL NUEVO DIARIO
Alan a Nicaragua
uspensiones en el PLI
o tienen fuerza legal

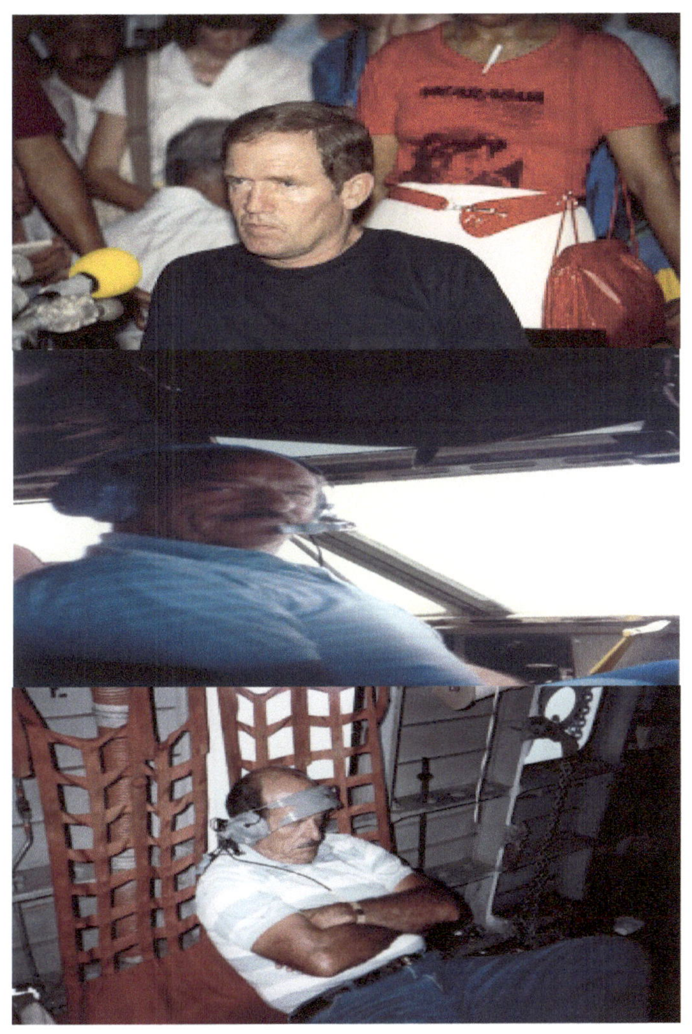

[MONTHS BEFORE]

(EXT. ILOPANGO AIRBASE ELSALVADOR - OCT 5, 1986 - C-123 CARGO

PLANE)

[Visual - fork lift loading camouflaged C-123 cargo plane. Dan, Nicky, Pilot and co-pilot are picking up their knapsacks and boarding the plane]

[Roll call in the background at the airport hangar]

TRANSPORT COORDINATOR

Chammorro? -- aqui!

Agudo? - ola!

Robel? - si!

Prado? - si!

Gomez? - aqui!

Calero? - [someone says] - no he is at the camp!

Pena? - [someone says] - he is in Miami!

North? [Someone says he is in Washington DC] Casa Blanca!

Ian Crawford? Don't know him!

Max Gomez? Don't know him!

Colonel James Steele? Same don't know him!

General Richard Gadd (ret.)? Not on the list!

Sawyer? He is in El Salvador!

Cooper? He's in El Salvador too!

Father Z?

William P. Goode=north
Mr. Steele Hammer=north
Barnaby, ac or sparkplug
Spitz channell
Rich miller
One eye - haskel/olmstead HR Block

[Plane takes off down the run way and up into the air]

[A Russian-made SAM-7 surface-to-air missile launcher]

SANDINISTA SOLDIER 1 (TO SANDINISTA SOLDIER 2)

[In spanish] Listen you hear that - they are coming to make a drop. Quick help me aim.

[click - swooossssh] [At that moment, the young Sandinista fired his shoulder-mounted missile, whose Russian name "Strela" means "arrow]

PILOT (TALKING OVER PLANE HEADPHONES)

Guys get ready for the drop we are now in Nicaraguan airspace - altitude is 2,500 feet fast approaching San Carlos - up the Río San Juan.

DAN

[BSSSSSHKKKOOOMP WOOMP WOOOMP] Whoa! What the hell was that?

Unlike his colleagues, Dan and Nicky had parachutes since he listened to what the SOA Instructor had said about Risk and thinking out of the box.

SANDINISTA SOLDIER 2 (TO SANDINISTA

SOLDIER 1)

[in Spanish] Did you hit it? Did you get it?

SANDINISTA SOLDIER 1 (TO SANDINISTA SOLDIER 2)

[in Spanish] I don't know

NICKY

WE'RE HIT WE'RE HIT BAIL OUT

[Dan scrambles to put on his parachute. Nick hits the button for the cargo door to open]

NICKY

SEE YOU ON THE GOUND BUDDY - HOPE THE GALLO PINTO IS TASTY

[With the wind rushing in as the cargo door goes down both Dan and Nick run and leap off the ramp]

[On the way down Dan can hear gun fire. They are being shot at as they descend into the deep jungle bush] [Dan land s and begins to roll up the parachute to hide it. He sinks his hand into the mud and wipes it on his face to darken his appearance]

DAN (WHISPERING)

[tip toeing thru the jungle] Nick? Nick? Nick where are you?

[Dan stepping over branches]

[Dan's getting desperate] **DAN (WHISPERING)**

Nick? Come on - where the hell are you? Show yourself?

[Dan looks to his left and then up - Nicky appears dead from a gunshot wound and his parachute is stuck 15 feet up on a branch so he is just dangling in the air]

DAN (WHISPERING)

Oh man - Nick what the hell happened?

[all the lower branches are cut off and there is no way to climb up] [Dan wants to cut him down but can't reach] [Gunfire is getting close] [Holding his head he slides down the tree trunk as a slight rain mist begins]

Talking Heads Music fades in:

"Heaven"

Everyone is trying to get to the bar.
The name of the bar, the bar is called Heaven.
The band in Heaven plays my favorite song

[Gunfire is getting close]

[To destroy any ID Nicky may have on himself - Dan takes out a flare gun and aims it up the tree at Nicky]

NICK (WHISPERING)
I ain't dead yet.
[Gunfire is getting closer]

DAN (WHISPERING)
Farewell my friend. You will be missed

[Dan pulls the trigger]

[As Sandinista soldiers approach Dan shoots flares up in the air over Nick's body so they can find his body [to return to U.S.A. in a later Sandino prisoner swap with the rebels in exchange for Nick's body]
[Dan stops and puts on his hearing aid and listens. Takes his hearing aid off and catches his breath] [He can sense someone is near and can detect branch/twigs snapping]
[Dan also lays two booby traps (trip wires to flare guns) to slow down the Sandinos]

[whooosh as the flare take off]

[Dan begins running through the jungle]
Rob Zombie - Dragula Lyrics (Jungle Run - Nicaragua)

[Use Australian SAS - TheWitchFinderZ13 Version]
Dead I am the one, exterminating son
Slipping through the trees, strangling the breeze
Dead I am the sky, watching angels cry
While they slowly turn, conquering the worm

Dig through the ditches,
And burn through the witches
And slam in the back of my Dragula

Dig through the ditches,
And burn through the witches
And slam in the back of my Dragula

Dead I am the pool, spreading from the fool
Weak and want you need, nowhere as you

bleed
Dead I am the rat, feast upon the cat
Tender is the fur, dying as you purr

Dig through the ditches,
And burn through the witches
And slam in the back of my
Dragula

Dig through the ditches,
And burn through the witches
And slam in the back of my
Dragula

Do it baby, Do it baby
Do it baby, Do it baby
(Burn like an animal)

Dead I am the dog, hound of hell, you cry
Devil on your back, I can't never die,
I can't never die...
I can't never die!

Do it baby, Do it baby
Do it baby, Do it baby
(Burn like an animal)

Dig through the ditches,
And burn through the witches
And slam in the back of my
Dragula

Dig through the ditches,
And burn through the witches
And slam in the back of my
Dragula

Dig through the ditches,

Just Dan takes off running and before the Sandino forces reach Nicky up in the tree American Delta Forces were also hiding nearby. They scramble to get to Nicky's location to find out if he is an American shot down. Dressed in full tactical gear covered by branches and leaves they sneak up on Nicky.

WHITE DELTA FORCE (WHISPERING)
Hola Amigo.
[Gunfire is getting closer]

NICKY (WHISPERING)
Hey hey get me down from here.

WHITE DELTA FORCE (WHISPERING)
Usted Americano?
[Gunfire is getting closer]

NICKY (WHISPERING)
Yes yes I am American get me down from

here.

WHITE DELTA FORCE (WHISPERING)
Do you have rescue insurance?

NICKY (WHISPERING)
Yes yes I do hurry up get me down from here. They are coming.

WHITE DELTA FORCE (WHISPERING)
Do you have two forms of ID and a Drivers License?

NICKY (WHISPERING)
Well Yes I did but I had to destroy it for fear of being captured. Cmon guys!

WHITE DELTA FORCE 1 TO WHITE DELTA FORCE 2 (WHISPERING)
He ain't got no rescue insurance come on lets go.

BLACK DELTA FORCE 1 TO WHITE DELTA FORCE 2 (WHISPERING)
Guys you gonna leave a brother up there like that? Mannnn that just ain't right. Whatz a brother gotta do to get a ride home??? (picking up gear and leaving)

[Day 29 Dan is still surviving in the jungle - he is full beard - raggity dirty]

[As Dan is walking through the jungle he passes an open area - stops and takes one step]

[Whossh a trap net catapults Dan up and dangling 10 feet in the air - Dan is swearing in English]

[No sooner Dan is caught in the net - he uses his knife to cut his way out]

[Falls out of the net and lands on his feet - looks up and a very huge camouflaged man grins with black teeth - Dan hits him and runs only to be grabbed again by 3 huge guys]

TALL/HUGE MERCENARY GUY 1 (TALKING OUTLOUD COVERED IN MUD AND CAMO MAKEUP)

Where are you going AMERICAN BOY?

TALL/HUGE MERC GUY 2 (TALKING OUTLOUD)

Yes it is not nice you are a bit rude. Hang out with us

DAN
Are you guys American?

HUGE MERC GUY 1 (TALKING OUTLOUD)
Yes American Boy just like Apple Pie?

HUGE MERC GUY 2 (TALKING OUTLOUD)
Come we will get you out of here.

DAN
(Dan is not so sure with all the cammo make up] (in disbelief)Barry is that you?

HUGE MERC GUY 2 (TALKING OUTLOUD)
Dan? What the hell what are you doing in the middle of the jungle getting chased by Sandista soldiers? Come meet the rest of the guys - you going to blow their minds. You look like a fricken chameleon

[Walking towards the U.S./commando base camp.]

[Just like the old days - Dan tells all his friends that joined the Marines about what happened -music is playing. Visuals - guys eating, talking joking, camp fire]

HUGE MERC GUY 2 (BARRY)
Dan I have someone that wants to meet you - presenting Seniorita Estalita [Estalita is a splitting resemblance of Stephanie - causing Dan to remember she has no idea what happened to him] Dan that's Nelson over there - check out his babe. Now where the hell is our cook Marcarena? I AM STARVING!!!

HUGH MERC GUY (BARRY)
MARCARENA WHERE ARE YOU???

MARACRENA

MARCARENA

[The song kicks in and the most beautiful big breasted, bubble butt, athletic looking Latino women in various scraggly but scantily clad almost nude go to the center of the camp a begin the MACARENA dance while the guys stare in awwww]

I am not trying to seduce you)

When I dance they call me Macarena
And the boys they say que estoy buena
They all want me, they can't have me
So they all come and dance beside me

Move with me, chant with me
And if you're good I'll take you home
with me

set ena pol and a hena macarena
h and a so onapeeda
set en a pol an a hena macarena
Hey Macarena!
(Ay!)

set ena pol and a hena macarena
Que tu cuerpo es pa' darle alegria cosa
buena
set ena pol and a hena macarena
hey macarena!
(Ay!)

Now don't you worry about my boyfriend
The boy who's name is Vitorino
Ha! I don't want him, can't stand

Dale a tu cuerpo alegria, Macarena
Hey Macarena!
(Ay!)

(Ay! Ay!)
(Ay! Ay!)
(Ay! Ay!)
(I am not trying to seduce you)
(Ay!)

M-M-Macarena
M-M-Macarena
M-M-Macarena
(Ay!)

M-M-Macaren

[Just then a monkey pulls the trigger on an AK-47 and everyone runs for cover]

DAN

Happy Thanksgiving guys!

DAN (TO BARRY AND GROUP)

Wow shes beautiful! But guys I know you are thinking of me - I really have to get back to Miami.

[Dan kisses Estalita on her on cheek]

HUGE GUY 2(BARRY)

If you gotta go you gotta go!! Grab your

stuff because that convoy is headed to a supply helicopter that can drop you in Miami. FAREWELL AMERICAN BOY!!!!!

[Dan says farewell and high fives all the guys and runs to the convoy]

END OF NIC

[FADES TO BLACK]

CHAPTER SIXTEEN

CUBA - FISH OR STEAK

Castro's Palace

[A jump forward from Matt Drudge's narration (Danny's dead body missing from the Vanishing Point van - scene #1 flashback). After the CIA blackmails Fidel Castro's lady doctor its Danny's big break "Access to Castro" The Doctor has agreed to pair the two for some important business discussions]
[View - entrance to room]

[Visual - man's shoes camera moves from feet/shoes upward - you see clearing security - Cuban guard is scanning Dan and Stephanie with metal detector wand by hand]Dan is carrying a large chocolate cake - a gift for Castro. Security man scans the cake]

[Both Dan and Stephanie are greeted by Castro.] [Proceed into a very large state dining room]

CASTRO
Welcome! welcome! Dra Briceno has told me a lot about you. Please join me for lunch.

DAN
Thank you! Thank you for having us. This is my best friend and assistant BETSY STUWAY.

[STEPHANIE (ROLLING HER EYES ABOUT HER MISTAKEN NAME INTRO) (SHAKING CASTRO'S HAND)]

DAN
A pleasure, thank you for having us.

[A FEW OTHER GUEST ARRIVE AND ARE GREETED BY CASTRO BEFORE SITTING DOWN AT THE SAME TABLE]

CASTRO
Please come this way (seating Dan and Stephanie side by side). Please tell me what is your preference Steak or Fish?

[Unarmed Danny is searching the room for a weapon. Then and " Aha moment!"]

DAN
We will both have steak well done.

STEPHANIE
[Stephanie whispers to Dan - it is good to see you didn't bring any weapons today]

No, no, no I will have fish. Please make mine fish. Fish of the day. Thank you.

[As the guest begin to settle in and dine. Castro begins talking in broken English. Castro's translator talking as fast as Castro]

[Camera flash to Castro's mouth, flash to translators mouth, flash to Dan and Steph, flash loop to all]

TRANSLATOR
As a result of rumor and speculation and innuendo, I have been accused of almost every crime imaginable. Wild rumors have abounded. Some have said I was guilty of treason and suggested in front of my daughter that I should be given the death penalty. Some said I stole 10 million

dollars. Some said that I condoned drug trafficking to generate funds, or that I personally ordered assassinations, or that I was conducting my own foreign policy. WHO DO THEY THINK I AM? NOREIGA?

DAN [WHISPERING TO STEPHANIE]

[Under his breath] What makes you think I came here to do anything???

[As food is served Stephanie picks up Dan's steak knife and places it away from his reach. Not wanting to alarm Castro Dan doesn't ask for the knife. Each time Stephanie picks it up to cut her food she puts it back on the table near Dan. Just as he reaches for it she snatches it up again. Dan keeps talking gibberish to Castro while eyeing the knife. Castro picks up on Dan's intent and starts choking on his lunch. Just then…….]

DAN (TO STEPHANIE)

GIVE ME THAT KNIFE!!!

STEPHANIE

No! You are not screwing up my lunch today!!

DAN

GIVE ME THAT KNIFE!!!

STEPHANIE

No! Not today honey I'm sorry but if you invited me for lunch aka assassination then you is crazy. Don't ask me to come here and then wreck the whole lunch - this food is pretty good.

[With all the commotion going on Dan begins to panic. Stephanie picks up the steak knife and throws it across the room. Not wanting to fail his mission Dan picks up a very large cake and smooshes it in the already choking Castro and then bolts to the door knocking over Stephanie, the servants, and body guards. Stephanie gets up and starts to run.]

CASTRO [LICKING CAKE OFF FINGERS]

Hmmmm its good -taste really good

[Beard hair starts falling out]

<u>EXT. CUBA - PRESIDENT'S PALACE – 1:30PM</u>

[Already out of the palace Dan is running as fast as hell. Exiting from the palace door Stephanie is yelling and chasing after Dan.]

STEPHANIE

WAIT! WAIT! Wait up for me……

[Right behind Stephanie exiting from the palace door are the out of shape body guards. One guard take out his pistol and fires a warning shot in the air. Stephanie falls [in slow motion]and Dan thinks she is shot.

STEPHANIE

Wait up for me……Don't leave me!

[Dan turns around and begins to run toward her as she is crawling with one hand in the air. Realizing she is not shot he grabs her hand (SLOW MOTION) and begins to undo a very large gold and diamond bracelet.]

STEPHANIE
What are you doing?

DAN
(DAN REMOVING THE BRACLET)
You won't be needing this anymore. You tried to keep me out of the military, out of the CIA, you almost got me killed! ANNNNND you screwed up my Castro mission. I am MYSTiFIED BY YOU!!!!!!!!!

That's it! That's it! - I am finished being your ex-boyfriend. This is the VANISHING POINT --- I quit!!

[Elian Gonzalez walking by]

Dan
Hey Elian Gonzalez - High Five

[From a distance camera view]

[Dan turns and runs down to the beach uncovers a buried bag - straps on a jet pack to his back, drags a wind surf board to the water - clicks the jet pack on and holds the sail of the wind surfboard. He goes like a jet on the surface of the water out towards the ocean until he fades away. The soldiers stop and pick up Stephanie. Dan has escaped the soldiers and body guards.]
(Fade in Song: American Boy - Estelle feat, Kayne West)

THE END

[Movie credits begin]

Beat - 2nd song begins

"Life During Wartime"

Heard of a van that is loaded with weapons,
packed up and ready to go
Heard of some gravesites, out by the highway,
a place where nobody knows
The sound of gunfire, off in the distance,
I'm getting used to it now
Lived in a brownstore, lived in the ghetto,
I've lived all over this town

This ain't no party, this ain't no disco,
this ain't no fooling around
No time for dancing, or lovey dovey,
I ain't got time for that now

Transmit the message, to the receiver,
hope for an answer some day
I got three passports, a couple of visas,
you don't even know my real name
High on a hillside, the trucks are loading,
everything's ready to roll
I sleep in the daytime, I work in the nighttime,
I might not ever get home

This ain't no party, this ain't no disco,
this ain't no fooling around
This ain't no mudd club, or C. B. G. B.,
I ain't got time for that now
Heard about Houston? Heard about Detroit?
Heard about Pittsburgh, P. A.?
You oughta know not to stand by the window
somebody might see you up there
I got some groceries, some peant butter,
to last a couple of days
But I ain't got no speakers, ain't got no headphones, ain't got no records to play

Why stay in college? Why go to night school?
Gonna be different this time
Can't write a letter, can't send a postcard,

This ain't no party, this ain't no disco,
this ain't no fooling around
I'd like to kiss you, I'd love you hold you
I ain't got no time for that now

Trouble in transit, got through the roadblock,
we blended with the crowd
We got computer, we're tapping phone lines,
I know that ain't allowed
We dress like students, we dress like housewives,
or in a suit and a tie
I changed my hairstyle, so many

[FADES TO BLACK]

THE END

ABOUT THE AUTHOR

No comment.

THE WHITE HOUSE

North was there as *contra* leader Calero presented Reagan with an I'M A CONTRA TOO pin

How Iran-Contra Unfolded

Dec. 1, 1981 President Reagan signs "finding" authorizing CIA assistance for *contras* in Nicaragua.

May 21, 1983 State Department launches Operation Staunch to discourage sale of arms to Iran by other nations.

April 6, 1984 *Wall Street Journal* exposes CIA mining of Nicaraguan harbors as Reagan lobbies for $24 million in *contra* aid.

Oct. 12, 1984 Third and most restrictive of Boland amendments forbids all U.S. intelligence agencies to support the *contras*.

March 16, 1985 Associated Press bureau chief Terry Anderson is kidnapped in Beirut.

July 18, 1985 Reagan approves Iran initiative in meeting with Robert McFarlane at Bethesda Naval Hospital.

Sept. 14, 1985 Shipment of 408 TOW antitank missiles goes from Israel to Iran (96 were shipped on Aug. 20). Next day, hostage Benjamin Weir is released.

Nov. 24, 1985 U.S. HAWK missiles bound for Iran arrive in Israel.

Jan. 22, 1986 Iranian arms merchant Manucher Ghorbanifar proposes "diversion" of profits from Iran arms sales to *contras*.

April 4, 1986 North, in message to Poindexter, proposes diverting $12 million in Iran arms profits to *contras*.

May 25, 1986 McFarlane, North and others arrive in Tehran to negotiate sale of arms and release of hostages.

Sept. 25, 1986 Congress okays $100 million in lethal and nonlethal aid to *contras*.

Oct. 5, 1986 Plane carrying American Eugene Hasenfus and 10,000 lbs. of arms is shot down in Nicaragua.

Nov. 2, 1986 Hostage David Jacobsen released following shipment of 500 TOW missiles to Iran.

Nov. 3, 1986 Story from Beirut magazine *Al Shiraa* describing McFarlane's trip to Tehran reaches U.S. press.

Nov. 13, 1986 On nationwide TV, Reagan denies he traded arms for hostages.

Nov. 25, 1986 Reagan and Attorney General Ed Meese announce discovery of "diversion," resignation of Poindexter and firing of North.

Dec. 19, 1986 Lawrence Walsh appointed special prosecutor.

July 7-14, 1987 North testifies under immunity before Iran-*contra* committee.

March 16, 1988 Special prosecutor Walsh indicts North.

May 4, 1989 North convicted on three counts, acquitted on nine.

Sept. 16, 1991 Walsh drops all remaining charges against North after court rules that testimony of key witness McFarlane was tainted by his exposure to North testimony given under immunity.

PROPOSED MYSTiFYED BY STEPHANIE SOUNDTRACK

1. "Cities (Talking Heads)" – 0:00
2. "Burning Down the House (Talking Heads)" – 0:00
3. "Camp Town Ladies" (Acapella) – 0:00
4. "City of Dreams (Talking Heads)" – 0:00
5. "Can I Get A (Jay Z)" – 0:00
6. "Gorillas (Feel Good, Inc.) " – 0:00
7. "Bad! (Michael Jackson)" – 0:00
8. "Please Don't Leave (Pink)" – 0:00
9. "Nothing But the Flowers (Talking Heads)" – 0:00
10. "Psycho Killer" (Talking Heads) – 0:00
11. "Road to Nowhere" (Talking Heads) – 0:00
12. "Life During Wartime" (Talking Heads) – 0:00
13. "This Must Be the Place" (Talking Heads) – 0:00
14. "Slippery People" (Talking Heads) – 0:00
15. "Tip Toeing Thru the Tulips" (Acapella Tiny Tim Impersonator) – 0:00
16. "Wild Wild Life " (Talking Heads) – 0:00
17. "Pulled Up" (Talking Heads)– 0:00
18. "Shut Up and Dance" (Walk the Moon) – 0:00
19. "Once in a Lifetime" (Talking Heads) – 0:00
20. "Heaven" (Byrne, Harrison) – 0:00
21. "Dragula" (Rob Zombie, Austrian SAS Version) – 0:00
22. "Marcarena" (Los del Río) – 0:00
23. "American Boy" (Estelle Feat Kayne West,) – 0:00
24. "Once in a Lifetime" (Repeat Talking Heads – during credits) – 0:00

1349

UNCLASSIFIED

~~TOP SECRET~~

Chapter Footnote 14-77

N 2801

Copp: 8/26/86 1320

261800Z Aug 86.

Partially Declassified/Released on 27 May 87 under provisions of E.O. 12356 By B. Reger, National Security Council

1. Following is summary report of three long meetings -- total circa eight hours -- with Iranian gp visiting Brussels. Meetings took place August 25 in three segments. Iranian side was [redacted] of Rafsanjani [redacted] Our side included me -- true name -- Abe in true name, and [redacted] our agent. Meetings constituted comprehensive tour de force regarding Iran/Iraq War, Iranian views of U.S. and other western policies, Soviet activities, activities of nearly all important Iran government figures, hostage matters, activities in the Hague, and Iranian forces equipment and materiel shortages.

2. Special interest items included claim that [redacted] have recently tried to meet with [redacted] -- he has declined -- he wants to deal with the Presidents representatives. [redacted] is very sharp, [redacted] speaks no English. [redacted] claims Rafsanjani now heads supreme war council and aims to terminate war but in little more favorable military situation for Iran than current. They badly need air defense items, armor spares, TOWs, gun barrels, helo spares, and [redacted]. I told them all things negotiable if we can clear the hostage matter quickly. [redacted] knew great deal about McFarlane man to Thn. He also knows all about [redacted] Gorba, Isareli connection, and this gps financial

~~TOP SECRET~~

UNCLASSIFIED

939

N1158 12/2/86 KL

1350

N 2802

~~TOP SECRET~~

2

greed. Gorba was nastly classified as a crook. ████ wealth of current of information but also volunteers to discuss hostage matter and USG connection with ████ in next 10 days. He will then return to Brussels for meeting with us. ████ said categorically he would not screw up ████ efforts but would carefully examine them for feasibility. ████ will recommend two courses to ████

a. Assist in current ████ effort to release hostages or start new effort.

b. ████ says there are many specific things USG can do in the Hague and on Voice of America programming to help start USG/GOI talks -- he will give us documents on these subjects at next meeting.

3. Numerous military supply problems were discussed and I will detail these for you later this week in Washington. FYI: They need oil barter deals.

4. My judgement is that we have opened up new and probably much better channel into Iran. This connection has been effectively recruited and he wants to start dealing. Recommend you plan on bringing George to next meeting in two weeks or less.

Rgds, Dick. BT

~~TOP SECRET~~

"Two reasons," he replied. First, all Nicaraguan bank accounts in the U.S. had been frozen. Second, the Treasury Department monitors large transfers of funds in and out of American banks. Someone was bound to notice these transactions and start asking questions.

"You're Talking Too Much"

In February 1985, King Fahd of Saudi Arabia arrived in Washington on a state visit. During his meetings with the President, he agreed to provide additional funds to the resistance. When the money began to arrive, Calero used it to buy weapons and supplies. He often called me for advice, and soon we conferred about everything, from where the *contras* could buy surface-to-air missiles to the need for more obstetricians in the base camps.

DENNIS BRACK—BLACK STAR

Casey told North, "Shut it down and clean it up"

One afternoon, Casey called me from his office at the Intelligence Community Staff Building on F Street. "Can you come over and see me right now?"

I threw on my coat, ran over to F Street, and took the creaky old elevator to Casey's office. He said, "You're talking too much."

"What do you mean?"

"On the phone. How often are you talking to your pal in Honduras? Three, four times a week?"

"Something like that."

"All in the clear, right?"

"Yes."

"Well, it's got to stop." Casey said these calls made it too easy for the Soviets to listen in on my talks with Calero. He handed me a small black book with a series of little pockets inside. "Have you ever used one of these?"

"No. How does it work?"

He shook his head, as if to say, Do I have to explain everything? "It's a code book," he said. "You get one, he gets one. You change the code numbers on a set pattern. Now you can talk without giving away the store."

All you had to do was enter the relevant words—Honduras, Nicaragua, guns, ammo, medicine, planes—then line them up with the code numbers in the book, which could be changed every day. It was low-tech but effective. Somebody listening in would have virtually no idea what you were talking about.

Later, when more people were involved in our contacts with the resistance, Casey called me in again. "What are you doing about security?" he asked. "Your COMSEC [communications security] stinks." Casey was concerned about the Soviets' ability to monitor calls from their listening post in Lourdes, Cuba. What had begun as a simple link between Adolfo and me soon involved more than a dozen people on at least two continents. Adolfo and I were still using the original code books, but that didn't protect the others. Casey recommended a new, American-made encryption device manufactured by TRW, the KL-43.

The code books and communications equipment may have helped keep the Soviets and the Cubans from knowing the details of what I was doing to support the resistance, but the secret kept spreading. There must have been well over 100 people in our government (including State, Defense, CIA, the White House and Congress) who knew at least some of what was being done. As the CIA phased out and I became the focal point for the resistance, we tried to tighten that circle. But for a covert operation, there sure were a lot of people who knew about it—at least until the great plague of amnesia that hit Washington in the fall of 1986.

As the summer of 1984 came to an end, I felt as if I were straddling a canyon. On one side was the resistance, always expanding, always needing more. On the other was the CIA, which was steadily withdrawing its support. The canyon was growing wider by the day. Un-

About That Cake . . .

In November 1986, when the world learned of our visit to Tehran, it was widely reported that we brought a Bible signed by President Reagan and a cake in the shape of a key—to symbolize our desire to open a new relationship with Iran. The report about the Bible was wrong. But we did bring a cake. It was not, however, in the shape of a key. Moreover, it had no real connection with our mission.

Manucher Ghorbanifar, our channel to the Iranians, had asked that we bring a cake as a gift for his aging and widowed mother, who lived in Tehran. Because that was one of Gorba's easier requests, Amiram Nir and I bought a large, rectangular chocolate layer cake at a kosher bakery in Tel Aviv. Aboard the plane, I carefully laid the cake box on the sink in the galley. During the flight, when I opened the cabinet above the sink to look for coffee cups, I noticed the matched sets of pistols we had brought as gifts on the same shelf as the dishes. Each set of pistols was packed in an elegant case with a handsome brass key.

As I reached for the cups, one of the keys fell onto the uncovered cake, making a sizable indentation. When I saw how deeply the key had fallen, I left it there, hoping it would look like an intentional decoration. "Well," I said to a colleague, "we can always tell Mrs. Ghorbanifar that this is the key to our hearts."

Ghorbanifar's gift never reached his mother. When Nir and I wandered down the hall of the Tehran Hilton, several of the revolutionary guards were playing with the pistols . . . and eating the cake.

11

Copp: 4/11/86 1000

101450Z Apr 86. L-100 arrived over DZ on time but never saw inverted L or strobe lite. They remained in area 25 minutes and then aborted. Ralph coordinating with who says troops saw and heard L-100. I want to try again tonight an hour earlier but Steele has informed Ralph that he will not permit another "half ass" operation. He says we have to establish air/ground radio contact before he will permit op to go forward. This is assinine -- no black ops ever use this procedure. The answer is to sort out why the troops did not have signals properly displayed, including most importantly the strobe lite. Also Sat wants their bird back. I will handle Sat if you take care of Steele. This must be done right away or we must return the bird. Rgds, Dick. BT

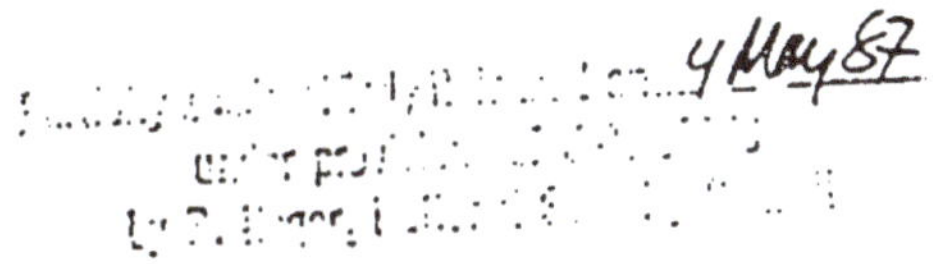

www.ingramcontent.com/pod-product-compliance
Lightning Source LLC
Chambersburg PA
CBHW041126100726
47911CB00002B/50

9780692160329